HTRAE
Assignment — Operation Earth Angel

❧ *Htrae* ❧

Assignment –
Operation Earth Angel

Elizabeth MacDonald
Burrows

Sense of Wonder Press
JAMES A. ROCK & COMPANY, PUBLISHERS
ROCKVILLE • MARYLAND

Htrae: Assignment — Operation Earth Angel
by Elizabeth MacDonald Burrows

SENSE OF WONDER PRESS
is an imprint of JAMES A. ROCK & CO., PUBLISHERS

Address comments and inquiries to:
SENSE OF WONDER PRESS
James A. Rock & Company, Publishers
9710 Traville Gateway Drive, #305
Rockville, MD 20850
E-mail:
jrock@rockpublishing.com   lrock@rockpublishing.com
Internet URL: www.rockpublishing.com

ISBN: 1-59663-529-0
978-1-59663-529-6

Library of Congress Control Number: 2006931634

Printed in the United States of America

First Edition: 2007

Dedicated to

Professor Edmond Bordeaux Szekely...
who encouraged me to write this book,
and who was also my inspiration for
the character of Professor Biogenics

Also to

The young of heart
who seek answers to the
mysterious riddle of life and
the secret of the stars

And

The wise for whom
there is a tender revelation
which holds a hope
for all mankind.

My deep appreciation to the following people
who joined me during the adventure of writing Htrae

Joe Tucciarone
for allowing his beautiful artwork
to be used for this cover.

And

Janet Bergland
Drucilla Briggs
Benjamin and Judith Godair
Peter Hiatt
Santosh Kumar Boddekuri
Sandra Lundstrom
Rene Maurer
Nancy Potts
Mary Ransdell
Michael Shemet
Cheryl Watkins
Keith Wong

TABLE OF CONTENTS

INTRODUCTION

Ridendo dicere verum ... my old friends, the Romans, had a proverb for everything, and "to tell the truth laughing," is a good way to describe the message in this book. It is a charming tale, full of laughter and joy, but also truth. Sapiete sat ... "a word to the wise is sufficient."

Therefore, I wish you Bon Voyage as you embark on these pages into a special world peopled by strange beings, which resemble all of us. If you feel that there is an important message hidden in these curious adventures, then I remind you of another of my favorite Roman proverbs: *Bene vixit qui bene latuit* ... "He who hides well, lives well."

—Professor Edmond Bordeaux Szekely

FOREWORD

The idea for *Htrae* was first conceived for children. However, it contained far too many of the mysteries of life to remain so. When those who read the original material came to me and said, "This is one of my favorite books," I began to realize that people wanted simple answers to the riddle of day-to-day existence — Where do we go when we die? What is our purpose for being? Will we have peace on Earth? What are angels?

Finally, I took the original manuscript and began to modify it so that all people, both young and old, could enjoy a journey into the unknown without dull religious, philosophical, or scientific analysis. My own reward for this task has been a wonderful journey into a land of happy people where there is no crime, violence, or war.

Htrae's very unusual family, better known as Starians, has introduced me to many new friends, such as Sir Cellular, Master Ether, Gusty, and Ambassador Marius. Through my visits with them, I have developed a greater love for all things, particularly for people and trees. And even now, the Starians' favorite tree friend, Brother Arbo, smiles at me from my back yard, while Gusty plays hide-n-seek between the world we see and the world that we do not see.

Although some people feel that Earth will never become a planet of peace, I believe in the mission of Htrae. If our planet were not really on a path of progression, there would be no hope for a better tomorrow and our ancestors would become no more than a few written pages in some history book. However, in this vast universe with billions of galaxies giving birth to suns and planets, there appears to be a system. If this is so, then Earth is destined for a greatness now beyond the comprehension of mankind.

My wonderful friends, the Starians, have all graduated and departed for a rendezvous with destiny. I am confident that a little part of them will always live in the hearts of those who read their adventure. It is with many tender memories, I lay my pen aside and wait for that day in Earth's future, when humanity looks toward the stars and realizes that heaven is its true home. When this occurs, somewhere, far beyond the galaxies, Ambassador Marius and Master Ether will lay out Earth's Angel Robes.

—Elizabeth MacDonald Burrows

CHAPTER I

Origin of Htrae

T he winds of the vast cosmos once moved across a dark sea of unknowingness. In this unremembered period, the formlessness of a single consciousness stretched across infinity without boundaries or limitation. In time this consciousness became known as the Lord of the Stars, and it was he who established a great plan to fill the vacuous space with life. As the eons passed, the light of the Lord's consciousness produced neutrons, protons and electrons, which constantly collided and merged in chordal dance.

Millenniums moved through the ethers, and within their movement a great phenomena occurred. Forms rose up out of the mist and huge suns materialized to adorn the ebon robes of the formless. It was the beginning of creation — the birth of the galaxies.

Creation endowed the cosmos with magnificent rivers running to meet depthless seas, emerald trees stretching their branches toward the stars, and huge mountains covered with glistening diamonds to pay homage to the heavens. It was, however, the planets, which gave the greatest joy to the Lord of the Stars. These produced humans who walked upright and toiled amid the forests and swamps to survive, and the Lord loved the humans for they were his children. Some were tall and some were plump, while others had many arms and several eyes. Yet he watched over all of them for they were of him, although most had little remembrance of the days during the great abyss when they had not known separation.

Sometime, during the fruition of the *Great Plan*, the Lord of the Stars became deeply concerned over one of the smaller planets in his universe. It was extraordinarily beautiful, for it was covered with seas that touched every solid land mass. Its rivers were filled with amazing life forms and its soil produced an array of life-giving benefits that sustained all living creatures upon its surface. It was called Earth.

The planet Earth had now reached the third orbital rotation pattern around its parent sun and successfully passed through all of the phases of planetary progression, even producing human life. In the planet's beginning there had been many trials, for it came into existence through volcanic eruptions, molten lava flows and sulfuric rains. As the atmosphere changed, the rains, no longer sulfuric, cooled the surface of the planet and a living green substance called vegetation touched great water masses called seas.

Although the surface of Earth had once coursed with moving life forms, and great hulks roamed the planet's surface, it, like all things, was subject to constant change. During the passing centuries the hulks eventually disappeared and other wild creatures dwelled in their place. Then, one day — the most remarkable creature of all appeared. These were called humans. It was the humans who tamed the wild land and built mighty cities with mountainous towers reaching to the sky. They also harnessed the energies of the electrons and protons, and in time they lit up the earth like the night sky.

Unfortunately, the humans, whom the Lord of the Stars endowed with both individuality and reasoning, had become submerged in a cloak of survival and worldly activities. Therefore, they now possessed little or no knowledge of their potentiality which had been formed in the distant stars, or that their destiny had been written when the creation of the universe began. They busily involved themselves in many things, some bad and others good. It was the bad, however, that concerned the ruler of the heavens.

The wars on Earth had brought death and destruction. It was not uncommon for one human to hate another, while others became violent, committing murders and robberies. This did not mean that the basic nature of the humans on Earth was bad, for the Lord of the Stars had planted a seed of good within each. And it was this good which was destined to lead the human beings out of suffering, illness and death one day.

Each millennium, as the Lord of the Stars watched over the people of Earth he became more and more concerned. A great work had been assigned the planet, but with its constant unrest it could not fulfill its purpose. Therefore, it would be necessary for the humans to graduate and become divine in order accomplish their purpose. This meant that they would have to leave human progression and ascend to the higher angelic regions, or in other words – become angels. Unfortunately, this produced a rather serious problem, for Earth was moving further out into space each day. If they did not graduate before their planet hit a nearby asteroid belt, the preconditions for life would cease to exist. Unfortunately, they would then have to remain in the unseen regions of the unmanifested until another planet in the solar system devel-

oped human form. Should this occur, the planet Earth would eventually become what it was in the beginning, atoms, neutrons and
protons. The Lord did not want this to happen, however, so he
sent for his chief administrator, Ambassador Marius, to discuss
the problem.

Ambassador Marius, primary litigation expert for the entire
universe, worked with all of the great leaders of the various planets. The Ambassador, of course, was very familiar with the solar
system in which earth was located. He had helped Master Kuthumi
of the Planet Neptune, Master Hilarion of the Planet Jupiter and
Master Centauri of the Planet Saturn through human life, and
again when life forms on their planets had become advanced civilizations without dense form.

The Lord of the Stars had appointed Ambassador Marius as
Chief Administrator during the early formation of the universe,
for the Ambassador was quick in carrying out his duties, extraordinarily intelligent and sufficiently developed to be one with the
consciousness of the Lord of the Stars. This made it possible for
Ambassador Marius to travel anywhere in the millions of galaxies
and carry out the Lord's wishes. Now, he was being called to con-
fer with the Lord of the Stars over the problem of earth's transformation from human to divine.

As soon as he received the call from the ruler of the universe,
the Ambassador immediately hastened through Stargate One to
the Sacred Garden. This was the most beautiful and wondrous
place in the universe, for it was comprised of light beyond all light
and its streets were paved with radiant streams emanating from
the stars. Overhead the circular movement of an exploding nucleus
of newborn solar systems formed a spiral galaxy, turning the garden into a creative phantasm beyond the scope of any wonder
existing in the known universe.

On arriving at the Sacred Palace Garden, Ambassador Marius
bowed low before the Lord of the Stars, and said, "I received your

call my Lord. As always it is good to be in your presence. Yet, I gather from your message that you are faced with a serious problem."

"It is good to see you also Ambassador," the Lord replied. "I fear the universe keeps me very busy, and because of this it seems that we spend very little time together."

Sighing, the Lord of the Stars turned his full attention to the problem at hand, "You are quite right, of course. At the moment I have a deep concern about the Planet Earth. I'm sure you are somewhat familiar with it because of your work with other planets in that particular solar system. You see, according to my Table of Potentiality, the humans on Earth are supposed to graduate and become divine within the next few millennia. Unfortunately, the planet is moving closer to an asteroid belt with each rotation. It could arrive there before the humans graduate and this would be a great disaster. The pre-conditions to sustain its life forms would then no longer exist and the progression of humans would have to be held until some other planet reached a suitable evolutionary phase to support them. As you well know, that could take millions of years."

"Have we not faced this problem before, My Lord?" asked the Ambassador. "It seems that I remember a similar situation on Quaron, which is in one of the neighboring solar systems.

"You are quite right Ambassador. You must remember, however, that our usual procedure did not work as well as I would have liked, and the transition from human to angel took more work than usual. While this would normally not make a difference, I fear that in Earth's case, the asteroid belt shortens our time allocation."

"Um ... m ... I see what you mean, my Lord."

The Ambassador was quiet for a while, but soon he lit up until he was almost as bright as the sun. This often happened to him when he was inspired by some great cosmic idea. "I believe have an idea that just might work. Instead of sending me to earth at this time, because I am but one consciousness, why not create a new planet, and instill in it the necessity to help in Earth's graduation.

"Don't you think that might be a bit risky Ambassador?" the Lord asked. "Every time a new planet creates individual life forms, those life forms become submerged in worldly ways and their true nature remains unrevealed until they graduate from human to divine. If I do this, I fear that the new planet might follow the path of its predecessors. That would accomplish very little."

"My Lord, perhaps we could change the venue somewhat. Instead of going in to help the planet during the last phase of solid progression, we could start at the beginning. That way I could make certain the new planet does not become isolated in worldly way. Naturally, I would call in some helpers, such as Sir Cellular and Professor Biogenics. I believe that, with their assistance, we could shorten the planetary evolutionary process by two-thirds. This should allow more than sufficient time to graduate the humans before their planet reaches the asteroid belt."

The Lord of the Stars nodded his head, as he reviewed the Ambassador's proposal. "Yes, I believe that is indeed an excellent idea. It is something that we have never tried before and it should be an interesting experiment. In fact, if this works, life forms upon the new planet could ultimately become your assistants and help other planets to graduate, such as Venus and Mercury.

The ruler of the universe paused for a moment before continuing, in order to think the matter over. During this time Ambassador Marius did not speak, for he knew the Lord would not wish to be disturbed while he was contemplating on such a serious matter.

After a brief interim had passed, the Lord spoke again, "Let's see, there is an incubation nebulae only a few hundred light years from Earth. The new planet could be nurtured there until it is ready to fulfill its mission. Of course it might actually be better to allow the Earth's sun serve as a surrogate mother. Then the fledgling planet would be within the same solar system. Little by little it could then move away from the surrogate without being caught in the gravity pull of those planets closest to sun, that is, until it came within a contact radius of Earth. This could greatly facilitate, as well as expedite its work."

The Lord of the Stars paused again in order to further consider the idea. At last, having made a decision, he spoke, saying, "Yes, I believe the latter to be the better idea."

With this part of the plan concluded, the Lord paused and looked at Ambassador Marius with a slight smile, "Since this is basically your idea, would you like to name the new planet?"

"Thank you for asking, my Lord. You do not know what an honor this is for me, not only to name the new planet, but to also be in charge of the project from the very beginning. Insofar as a name, there does seem to be only one that is truly suitable for this new emissary of heaven, and that is Htrae. In a sense it would become kind of a counterpart to Earth."

Ambassador Marius paused for moment and nodded his head, his eyes taking on a glow of expectation. "Yes," he added, "I do indeed believe this will prove a splendid challenge. By-the-way, do you know when you will begin?"

"Why not immediately?" asked the Lord. "I will see that Htrae originates before Earth makes another revolution."

Moments later a great wave of light swept through the cosmos. From Earth it looked like a gigantic solar explosion, greater than an atomic or hydrogen bomb. However, from Ambassador Marius' perspective it looked like billions of minute particles of light, a reflection of the same light that emanated from the Lord.

As the Lord of the Stars and Ambassador Marius watched the birth of the new planet, they nodded to one another, each indicating a sense of satisfaction over what they had witnessed. The

Ambassador was first to speak, "It appears that your plan has worked very well my Lord. However, the new planet appears rather small. Do you really think it can handle such an important mission as saving Earth?"

For a moment the Lord of the Stars thought about the question that the Ambassador had put before him. When he spoke, his words came slowly as though he was considering the matter very seriously, "I believe it will grow up to be as large as Earth. Although Earth is one of the smaller planets in our universe, look at what it has accomplished. Why, the humans have developed boats that move through the water like fish and airplanes that fly like birds. They read and write, assist nature in producing food for millions of souls who live on the earth's surface, and they have harnessed the water to create electricity and built spacecraft to travel to the moon."

Turning to look directly at Ambassador Marius, the Lord of the Stars added, "Besides the new planet will have you as their primary overseer and I have every confidence in you. In answer to your question, yes, I believe that the planet Htrae will fulfill its mission very well, and its family will reflect the highest principles of the universe."

Turning to look at the new planet, the ruler of the universe, said, "I must bid you farewell Ambassador, although I want you to know that the progress of both yourself and the new world, will always be known to me."

Bowing as the Lord of the Stars said goodbye, the ambassador replied, "Yes, my Lord, you always know." Then, with a bit of subtle humor, he added, "It would be quite hard, my Lord, for you to ignore even a single cell in your body."

On hearing the Ambassador's comment the Lord softly chuckled, for indeed all life was within him and He was within all life.

CHAPTER II

The Starian
Awakening

As the Lord of the Stars returned to the work of Creation, Ambassador Marius went in search of those who would help him prepare Htrae for its Earth mission. Even as he departed, life in the new world was beginning.

The sun, of course, was many times larger than the small planetary children to which it gave birth. It was necessary therefore, for the offspring of Htrae, who would become known as Starians because they came from the stars, to remain very close to one another lest they become over-exposed to the cold outer atmosphere which filled the empty space between planetary masses. As Htrae orbited within the parameters of their sun-home, occasionally the new planet was momentarily exposed to the vast and cold outer space. This was always a frightening experience for the

Starians, who felt the cold air penetrate their bodies comprised of particles of solar energy. Nothing looked as large to them as the universe with its billions of galaxies.

Other times, while the Starians were hibernating and nestled comfortably together, they sensed the Lord of the Stars' plan for them. During these periods they knew that they would have to leave the sun nebulae one day to fulfill their destiny. This, too, was of great concern to them, because they wondered if they could really build a planet. Neither did they wish to leave the security of the nebulae. When the vision of the Starians' destiny disturbed the protected world they lived in, they tried to tell themselves that such an experience was in the far distant future. On other occasions, they preferred not to think of it at all.

A few millenniums passed before the Htrae family began to develop a measure of independent life. From unity and knowing, to collective, although possessing a sense of individuality, they progressed toward that time when the external building of their planet would have to begin. When this occurred timelessness would cease, and the days and nights would be measured according to its journeys around the Sun. First, however, the Starians would find it necessary to enter solar school and learn the fundamental principles of the One Law that governed the universe, as well as understanding nature, a reflection of that One Law.

Solar School was, and is, a prerequisite for all newborn planets, for it instills the mysteries of creation within all potential individual life forms. It also implants each planet's purpose, for each one plays a different role in the universe of the stars. While Earth was in its incubation period it was programmed to become a great cultural center, even as Mars was to become a planet of great technology. Only by this combination, could all of the planets in the solar system make a perfect whole. One day these, having reached unity with one another, would then collectively manifest this perfection through a higher form of creation. Therefore, it was necessary that Htrae be prepared for its mission, although its mission was one of extraordinary uniqueness.

When any planet aligns itself with its purpose it becomes very powerful, for it is then one with the Law of the Lord of the Stars. This One Law is comprised of all that is good in the universe, and includes love, power and wisdom, as well as eternal life and peace. Violation or deviation from this indwelling perfection, through war, hatred or jealousy, only creates weakness, death and destruction. Therefore, every planet born, although in unknowingness, does contain its own particular role in the universal plan. Each is destined to follow its indwelling nature in spite of the adversities created by any independent life form upon its surface.

Since Htrae was being sent to help another planet graduate from human to divine, it was very important for them to remain unfettered by the dark unknowing of matter. Thus, their first lesson was to learn that they, as well as earth, were part of one great light. To learn this, they would study with Ambassador Marius who had been watching over the new planet from the time of its birth.

The first day of study was an exciting adventure for the Starians. They entered the solar class room and saw one of the most amazing sights they had ever seen, although they had seen little, except those times they got a glimpse of the vast universe of the stars. There, before them, stood Ambassador Marius. He was dressed in the robes of the night sky, while a massive hat in the form of a sun sat on his head. His eyes were the color of the sky and his beard and hair were white as snow. Every star in the robe twinkled like a tiny diamond, but the most amazing thing of all was his sun hat — for it glowed exactly like the sun. Because it was so bright it almost blanked out the features of the Ambassador's face.

Looking down upon his new students with a measure of amusement, Ambassador Marius, said, "I see that my hat is causing all of you a bit of a problem because of its brightness. So first, I will just turn it down a bit."

Watching in amazement, the Starians saw Ambassador Marius reach up and tweak a little tiny button on his hat. Immediately, the sun hat became a soft translucent glow, which no longer blinded them. They saw that his face was quite wrinkled, yet there seemed to be a gentle kindness about it. This gave him an appearance of being ageless, as well as possessing great wisdom.

When the Ambassador saw that his new students were over their surprise, he introduced himself, "I am Ambassador Marius and I have been sent by the Lord of the Stars, who has not only created, but also directs the Universe. It is my task to prepare you for your work with Planet Earth, who is in some ways your twin sister planet."

The Ambassador saw the quizzical looks on his students face when he mentioned that Htrae was in some ways related to Earth. After pausing for a moment he said, "I know that you will have many questions, so please do not hesitate to ask them. You see we will not only be together for quite an extended period, but we will also share in many experiences from now until your work with Earth is over."

By this time the Starians were filled with curiosity about Earth. They had heard this name whispered many times while they were in incubation and now their new teacher was also speaking about the matter. Even as they thought about asking Ambassador Marius concerning Earth, he spoke, "So you have been wondering about Earth?"

"It is well that all of you should know as much about earth as possible, for you will be hearing a great deal about it. Earth is known as a planet or a mass of ether and gasses which once lived here in the sun-home as you are now doing. Eventually, it moved into the colder outer space. Because of its intense heat, it was necessary for it to create an outer form to protect itself from destruction. At the time it contained the potential for a family, much like you. And, of course, little-by-little this potential developed into individual beings, or humans. As they did so, they unfortunately had no knowledge that they were also an integral part of the Lord of the Stars.

"This same Lord has now created you to help Earth. Their planet is moving toward an asteroid belt, which will destroy its' potential to sustain life if something is not done. It is, however, actually also time for them to graduate from human into divine. This will have to be accomplished before their planet collides with the asteroids. Unfortunately, the earthlings cannot really complete this task until they know who they are. Therefore, you have been assigned a mission by the Lord of the Stars, called, *Operation Earth Angel*. It will be your destiny to help the humans of Earth to discover who they really are, and to help them bring their planet to peace before the pre-conditions for life ceases to exist."

While all of this sounded very important to the Starians, they did not fully understand everything Ambassador Marius was saying. And thus someone asked, "Where do we start? What should we do?"

"It is too soon for you to fully comprehend the magnitude of *Operation Earth Angel*, but you will. Among the many things you will have to do is to build a planet, just as Earth has done. By doing so, you will better understand the long and difficult journey Earth has endured to become what it is. It happens that Earth is very beautiful and possesses blue seas, green hills and mighty mountains. You will eventually feel a deep love for it, because it is, in some ways, a part of you. For now, however, you must not allow *Operation Earth Angel* to occupy your mind, as there is much for you to learn before you can leave your home in the sun."

Ambassador Marius stopped talking for a moment. seemingly as though he was ready to take his leave. Then, almost as an afterthought, he looked intently at the Starians and began to speak again. "Although you may not understand this very well, Htrae has been created in such a manner as to develop more rapidly than ordinary planets because of the urgency of its unique assignment. At the same time, in order to understand Earth, you must also pass through all phases of planetary development."

Although the Starians did not really understand the Ambassador's statement concerning the acceleration of their planet, they felt a deep sense of apprehension when they heard that they would have to leave their home in the sun. Apparently the subtle awareness that had flowed through them during their incubation was to become a reality. Memories of their fleeting glimpses of the vast universe with its cold atmosphere filled them with dread. At the same time, they also felt something very deep and something very compelling, a desire to fulfill their assignment.

Ambassador Marius watched the Starians closely as he told them that they would have to leave the sun one day, and was aware of their deep concern. Yet, he had also seen the first faint flicker of responsibility for Earth's survival igniting the Starians' souls. He knew that this feeling would continue to grow throughout the growth of their planet. Because of this, he said, "It appears that you are ready to begin your training, so we shall begin."

"You can only build a planet in the solar system by working together. Just one of you alone would fail. The success of any planet depends on its people's ability to unite, for only then, are they true to their real nature. Every sun, and there are billions of suns like this one, as well as their planetary children, are of but one creation. This is evident because there is but one universe. Within the universe there are billions of galaxies and within the galaxies there are billions of solar systems. Yet, each still belongs to this one universe. Remember this always."

It was not long thereafter, it became a regular practice for the Htrae family to study with Ambassador Marius when part of their planet was turned away from the sun. They could then observe suns, or solar gods, being born and planets moving in their orbital positions within their individual solar systems. In time, it was obvious to the Starians that the universe was perfect and followed a systematic process of progression. The Ambassador had once explained that such perfection could only exist because all creation was within the body of the Lord of the Stars.

Little was mentioned during these happy times about *Operation Earth Angel*, but it was never far from the Starians' mind. They knew that it would not be long before they would have to leave the sun nebulae and move into outer space. By this time, individual personalities in some of the Htrae family started to develop. As this occurred, the Ambassador assigned the more advanced students personal names. Among these, Sebastian, who was always filled with questions about the mysteries of life. Then, afterward he would philosophize about the answers. Sometimes Sebastian would get so excited that his big, square glasses would jump up and down on his nose. He wore these because he wanted to see further and wider than one could see with regular vision. Besides they were a constant reminder that matter was created from the collective energy of four elements, earth, water, fire and air.

Other members of the Starians also received names. Ambassador Marius named Joan after Earth's great female crusader, Joan of Arc. Then there was Jason, who had an inclination toward music, and Webster, who showed a remarkable ability to put words into writing.

Next was Franklin, who was already interested in the possibility of uniting the atom in order to create a powerful energy source to help earth. He also thought that a grand unified theory might help explain that life came into being through a universal law of common attraction, or harmonics. Although Franklin did not know it, this concept was contrary to some of the research-taking place on Earth, for some scientists were more interested in splitting the atom. Yet, there were others who realized that the division of the atom would eventually lead to infinity, and such a discovery would prove that unity was the underlying principle of life.

The last two members of the Htrae family to receive names were Sally, who reminded the Ambassador of the beauty of nature, and Cedric, who showed an aptitude for art. Each would play an equally important, but different role, in the building of their planet. Collectively this made up the perfection of the whole. Even though the perfect prototype, or pattern, for the evolution of every living thing was within it, each independent life form still had to develop it. This meant that the greater work of Htrae, as well Earth, rested in its future. At the moment, Htrae was merely comprised of light, but this would change as the Starians became encased in dense bodies of matter.

During one of Ambassador Marius' classes, he said, "You have been taught that you will eventually take upon yourselves a cloak of matter, just as many planets have before you. Therefore, from the moment you leave here until you complete *Operation Earth Angel* your progression will be facilitated by what you learn. I cannot place too much emphasis on this; you must possess the ability to live harmoniously with all other life."

Of course, Sebastian then had to ask Ambassador Marius about the importance of the human bodies, because they had heard so much about them. It was their understanding that *Operation Earth Angel* would occur when the Htrae family reached that particular level of planetary progression, so they thought that must be very important.

Their teacher soon dispelled this theory by saying, "Human, or people bodies, are but a step in a long chain of soul progression, and after human bodies, there are subtle bodies made of semi-light. These subtle bodies never experience death or pain, but even so, each soul is still expected to pass into even higher states of planetary evolution. You see, life is always being born and life is always advancing in the billions of galaxies that make up the universe."

The Ambassador further clarified this theory during one of his subsequent classes, "In that the universe is one body and built out of one consciousness, the potential of everything exists even before it develops. If anything, including those who have developed people bodies, were completely free to follow an individual inclination, the universe would not be harmonious, but chaotic. The Lord of the Stars created the *Great Plan* of potentiality before the universe was brought into being. Although this may sound rather complex it is really quite simple. Imagine that you have a thought. As you think it, it ceases to become thought but a visible reality."

Of course this brought numerous questions to Sebastian's mind. It was somewhat difficult for him to perceive that everything really existed before it existed, so he asked, "We've been taught that there are things like wars on the planet Earth. From what we have learned, war means fighting one another and this brings separation. If everything is of one body, then why do they do this? It would seem that in fighting one another nothing is really accomplished, because everything is unity."

Ambassador Marius nodded to Sebastian, "You are quite right Sebastian nothing is really accomplished. Of course, at the time, those who war do not realize this. They believe they are accomplishing something. In a way, perhaps they are."

The Starians looked at the Ambassador, their eyes filled with curiosity. He smiled, "Let me ask you this and I want you to think about it. If everything is already one, then how can any real division exist? Ultimately, no matter how much anything is divided, it must eventually come to that point where further division is impossible. When division becomes impossible, then one discovers that everything was really one all the time."

On hearing this, Webster became quite excited, "Then it is true, if one were to take a single atom, like the substance we are made from, and divide it, and continue divide it, it would become more and more powerful because it becomes what it really is, the universe and beyond. Thus, the scientists of Earth would really touch infinity since there is no end.

"Yes, Franklin," Ambassador Marius replied, "they not only would discover infinity, but they will discover infinity. Then they will unlock the secrets of the universe."

On hearing the word secret, the Starians became even more curious, but their teacher knew only too well that one thing merely opened the door to another and there would be other times. Therefore, Ambassador Marius dismissed them for the day and left them to think, saying, "Life is both a school and a teacher. Anyone who becomes interested in studying and learning always speeds up the evolution of his or her particular world, as well as adding to their own individual growth."

CHAPTER III

The Universe
of the Stars

It was almost time for Htrae to move into its orbital pattern within the solar system. Because of this, the Starians were excited, although concerned. Outer space represented a cold and a vastness that differed much from their home in the sun nebulae. Yet, they were growing daily under Ambassador Marius' tutelage and could not help looking forward to the time when they would begin to fulfill their assignment. They were becoming more aware of the fact that their consciousnesses had expanded beyond the confines of their current existence. In spite of this, however, they were still very much involved in classes, although these were more advanced than their earlier studies.

During one of these classes, Ambassador taught, "Since the great plan of the Lord of the Stars lives within all life, all things reflect this perfect aspect. It is referred to as the *true nature*. While many of those who live on Earth are not actually familiar with their true natures, they can discover it through the practice of contemplation, of thinking. For instance, the sun reflects both the will and the love of the Lord of the Stars, for it shines on both rich and poor. Also, it contains the primary plan for the evolution and progression of its particular solar system. It must, therefore, not only create in the same manner as the Lord of the Stars, but must sustain all of the planets within its solar family.

"Because the planet Earth is already encased in matter, it produces many interesting things which you have not yet seen. For instance, they have birds that fly through the air to fill the day with song, and beautiful flowers that dance in the wind. There are trees that stand like stately sentinels and give protection to all things, even as they maintain ecological balance of their planet. Each of these are a reflection of their true nature because they are not endowed with the ability to reason, as are those encased in people bodies. Therefore, they do not have the capability of going contrary to their nature.

"One day, of course, all human souls must seek this true nature, and become it in order to graduate from human to divine. You will be there to help them. And you will see all these things I have spoken about as you develop your own planet."

Discovery of one's true nature puzzled the Starians, just as it had puzzled others throughout the history of the universe. Finally, Sally could not contain herself any longer and asked, "Ambassador Marius, please explain to us what you mean when you state that each must discover their true nature."

The Ambassador smiled at her and replied gently, "Sally, I fear that it is one of the great mysteries of the universe. In fact it is a question many people on earth are asking these days. To help you understand this, I want you to look at yourself and tell me exactly what you see."

"Well, I see me as a very bright light," Sally answered, "Actually; I seem to be exactly like the sun, only much smaller."

"Very good," commented the Ambassador. "It would appear then, that your true nature is like the sun, which in turn is a reflection of the Lord of the Cosmos. Without this nature you would not have the ability to become more. You would be exactly what you were before becoming a Starian. In other words, you could not even be Sally, because you would not exist.

"Now, Franklin," chuckled Ambassador Marius, "Tell me how you see yourself."

Franklin looked down at his body and was amazed to see that it had completely disappeared. "How did you do that?" he asked.

"That is a cosmic secret, but more important than seeing your outer physical self, explain to us exactly how you feel."

"Well, I feel lighter and no longer wish to remain within the sun. I wish to give life and create all things perfectly," Franklin replied. "It seems that I am less limited than when I was wearing my sun body."

"Very good, Franklin; that part of you is really like a cell, or an individual aspect, of the Lord of the Stars. It is this individual aspect of the Lord that will always cause you to strive toward greater accomplishments and to develop greater perfection. Even when you are not aware of this remarkable nature within you, you will continue to mold your planet into a greater and more advanced world because of it."

With this, the Ambassador blinked and Franklin looked down to see that he had returned to his sun-like body.

By this time the Starians were beginning to feel a strong inner urge to go forth and build a perfect planet, just like the souls of Earth. They knew that this feeling was natural, because the Great Plan of the Lord of the Stars flowed through them. Since a part of the Great Plan for Htrae existed within them, it was their plan also, and they could never really separate their consciousnesses from it. The Starians shook their heads in wonderment over this many times, for they realized that they would never really be alone, even if they became the furthest planet in the solar system. "Why," they thought, "If Earth really understood this, they would cease their disagreements and hostility because it isn't their true nature."

Even as the Htrae family prepared for their mission, rumors flew throughout the solar system that some of the people planets, including Earth, might not make it through their graduation from human to divine. Therefore, when the Starians heard this about their sister planet they could hardly wait to begin their work. "Little Emerald Planet," they whispered, their young voices floating through the ethers, "How we wish that you knew that the Lord of the Stars has not forgotten you, and that he loves you very much. Even now, he is asking us to leave our home here in the sun nebulae to help you. So, please – please never give up, for we will reach you in time."

One bright Starian morning Ambassador Marius sent a thought message to all of the members of the Htrae family to meet in the central sun classroom. Upon receiving his summons the family quickly hastened to obey. After taking their seats, they looked at the Ambassador questioningly.

Smiling, Ambassador Marius said, "The time has come for you to leave your home here in the sun and move out into the solar system so that you can build your own planet. Before you go, I want to advise you to do your work well and reflect the same ideal principle which exists throughout the universe of the stars. Also, I feel that I must remind you once more, to work together. If you do not, or if some of you try to become better than your brothers and sisters, your consciousness may become encased in the ways of matter. Unfortunately, you might then progress in unknowingness and without knowledge of who, and what, you really are.

"Although I will always be available to guide you in your work during the millenniums ahead, I may allow difficult things to happen to you. Thus, you must remember your early lessons here, yet be willing to learn new ones.

"When you leave your home here, it will be very cold. You are to snuggle tightly together and form a round ball. As the cold of the outer cosmos hits you, this combination of cold and heat will form rain. In turn the rain will help to cool your planet's surface and create a thick cloak of matter to protect you, as well as to provide all the preconditions necessary for your planet to sustain life."

After saying these words, Ambassador Marius paused for a moment and looked steadily into the eyes of the Starians. Finally he said, "I am afraid it is time for you to leave. Are you ready?"

Ambassador Maurius' announcement startled the Htrae family, even though they had been expecting it. They had only moments to look at their beloved teacher before the great sun door opened.

After the first initial shock, the Starians managed to focus their attention on the instructions that had been given them. They felt very small, as they looked out and saw millions of suns and countless solar systems. Nonetheless, without a moment's hesitation, but with many mixed feelings, they stepped out into the vast universe of outer space.

Suddenly the Starians found themselves falling at a very rapid rate, and for an instant they were afraid. However, before they had time to become too concerned, there was an abrupt jar and the falling sensation ceased. It became immediately apparent that they had landed in some kind of a cradle and, almost as immediately, they also realized that they had entered their own special orbital position in the Universe of the Stars.

Many days and nights passed, as the heat from the Starian light forms mixed with the cold of the outer cosmic sea. This caused great rains to fall, exactly as Ambassador had said, and soon their light bodies became hidden in a dark raincoat. In Earth time this took millions of years, but to the Starians this was but one day of cosmic time. Although they knew that this was the first step in building their planet, they were not aware that the heavy rains were creating floods and causing great landmasses to rise from the deep waters. These landmasses continued to congeal as the planet cooled, while of the lower places of Htrae retained the water and formed vast oceans.

Soon, the coat surrounding the Starians became heavier. Great mountains, caused by volcanic explosions, began to raise high above the surface of the planet. These explosions were none other than the solar core of Htrae, which had not yet been cooled or confined. Constantly expanding and constantly being subjected to the cold outer environment, the solar core of the planet continued to build. In time landmasses appeared everywhere, but as yet there were no trees or grass.

Later, as the process of progression continued, heat from the Starians caused a chemical reaction to occur between the elements. Originally there had been only two elements, fire and water. Now, however, as Htrae rotated in its orbital position, its motion caused both air and compression. This, in turn, resulted in producing matter capable of sustaining vegetation. Before long the azure skies and transparent seas of Htrae gleamed like a beautiful sapphire.

Deep beneath the surface of the new planet, gentle urges from the Lord of the Stars indicated that the more serious work of advanced growth must begin. Soon, the Starians began to feel very confined, but when they stretched something strange took place. They started to expand and, as they did so, they felt a cold, dark liquid penetrating every part of them. This caused such alarm that Sebastian decided that it was necessary to call a group meeting.

"Does anyone have any suggestions concerning our new situation?" Sebastian asked the group. "It appears that we may not be able to continue with the work that has been assigned us, because we seem to be trapped."

For a moment Sebastian paused, as if to think, then he said thoughtfully, "There simply must be a way out. Perhaps we are unable to find the solution because we spend our time talking about how frightened we are. Remember long ago when Ambassador Marius reminded us that the Lord of the Stars always lived within us? He also said that he, too, would watch over us. This must mean that both he and the Lord of the Stars are always ready to assist us. Perhaps it would be wise for us to contact the Ambassador."

"That is a wonderful idea Sebastian," Joan replied, "However, it has been a very long time since we left the solar nebulae and we have not had any contact with our teacher. I, for one, am not certain that I know how to reach him."

Sebastian looked at the others who had also gathered around him and said, "Joan has a point. I do have an idea, however, that might work. At least we can try it. Do you remember how Ambassador Marius used to call us together when he had something to discuss?"

"I do," Joan replied. "There would suddenly be an inner urge to go to the cosmic classroom, although Ambassador Marius never spoke a word."

"That is right," agreed Sebastian. "Therefore, I think the same thing might work for us. If we all think about Ambassador Marius at the same time, our consciousnesses might travel through space and reach him. Obviously, to do this, we must become as quiet as we were then."

The Starians huddled closely together beneath the surface of their planet without speaking. Each one thought about the Ambassador and their need for him. Almost immediately they heard his voice. It seemed to flow through them, much as it had done when they dwelled in the sun.

"Ah! And how are my little friends?" came Ambassador Marius' voice. "You probably think that I have been far away, but I really haven't. One thing about the universe is that time and space does not exist. Therefore, I have watched your development with great interest and knew that you would contact me when you were faced with a problem."

The delight of the Starians over meeting Ambassador Marius was obvious. The Ambassador, in turn, was pleased to be with them. "I see that you are concerned about the wet substance that seems to be enveloping your world. Actually, it is water. Remember when I told you about the rains, and that the rains would eventually help produce the pre-conditions for life on your planet? This has come to pass. As you hibernated within the confines of your newborn world, the rains descended and cooled the surface of Htrae. Now, there are great mountains and seas on your planet, just like those on Earth."

"Has all this really happened?" asked Sally. "You taught us that it would take many eons before these things would occur. Why, it doesn't seem very long at all."

"Well, Sally, you have actually been in space for a few eons," the Ambassador replied. "So you see, things progress swiftly when you are busy, but you also see how easy it is to forget. In all this time you really did not think of me at all, not that it was important for you to have done so. Nevertheless, this experience will help you to understand how easy it is for planets to get pre-occupied with outer things and lose all remembrance of their origin.

"At the moment it is very important for you to begin to experience your first real sense of individualization. You must stretch, or expand, and break free from the constriction that you feel."

"How are we going to do that?" Sebastian asked.

"It is really quite simple Sebastian. Breathe in deeply and fill your inner self from the atmospheric substance that surrounds you. Then allow your breath to go outward and feel yourself flowing with it. Very soon you will free yourself from the confines you are now in and discover that you are floating in water. It will feel somewhat like space, only heavier.

"Now, I must say goodbye and leave you to the work at hand. Remember, I am always one with your consciousness and therefore within immediate communication at all times. But, before I leave, I want to tell you that you will soon have a new teacher."

"But we don't want another teacher," cried Joan.

"Don't worry Joan," Ambassador answered. "I will always be your primary teacher, but there will be others. These will give you special instructions to aid you in building your planet. You will learn that there are some very remarkable instructors in this Universe of the Stars, although you need not concern yourself about that at the moment, for they will appear much later in your development. Among these are Sir Cellular and Professor Biogenics. Your first new teacher, however, is King Neptune, ruler of the seas. Although he is very interesting, you will probably find him somewhat strange at first."

Smiling at the group, Ambassador Marius said, "Unfortunately I must go, but we will be in contact many times over the centuries."

CHAPTER IV

The Undersea World of King Neptune

After Ambassador Marius withdrew his consciousness from their minds, the Starians settled down to the task of releasing themselves from the restrictions hindering their current progression.

Immediately Sebastian commented, "It seems that as we once left our home in the solar nebulae we must now leave this home. Otherwise there will never be life on Htrae. Although it appears that we have become a planet, it is apparently time for us to also become life upon it. Therefore, let us join hands and start breathing as Ambassador Marius suggested. I believe, if we allow ourselves to flow with our outgoing breath, we can move toward that light over there."

Holding hands and breathing in and out, with Sebastian as

their leader, the Htrae family soon felt themselves being pushed through a long dark passage. Before long they found themselves in the area from where a light seemed to be twinkling. Then, just as they had done when they had left the sun they stepped into the unknown.

Immediately, something caught hold of the Starians. It tore them apart, tossing them up and down and sideways. At first, Sebastian was unable see the others because it was too dark. Then he saw Joan, Franklin, Jason, Cedric and the others also bobbing around some distance away. They appeared like small specks of light.

"Ho, ho, ho," sounded a booming laughter. "You really are not doing very well, you know."

"Who are you, and where are you?" Sebastian called out. "It is impossible for me to see you, because it is very dark. However, I do hear you."

"I am King Neptune, ruler of the seas," a great voice roared. "You, and all your family, are now in the bottom of the ocean, Sebastian."

Such a statement immediately filled Sebastian with a number of questions, the first being, "How do you know my name?"

"I know all of your names," King Neptune replied. "Although you may not realize it, you have helped me create your ocean. Why, I have been waiting for you to appear for a very long time, but while I waited there was a great deal to do. First I had to find some means of providing food, so that you could survive when you changed forms."

About this time King Neptune held up some kind of a plant form. "Although none of you can see this, this is one of my greater endeavors. It is called seaweed. I know you will like the taste of it a great deal, although I admit it is a bit salty. Nonetheless it is not only tasty, but also a good purifier, particularly when it comes to radiation."

The king of the sea smiled a bit at this, "I know, I know, Sebastian, you are going to ask what radiation is, but that will have to wait. We have much more important things to attend to."

Sensing Sebastian's confusion, King Neptune chuckled, "Of course I know all about you. Ambassador Marius has been quite thorough."

While Sebastian was extraordinarily intrigued by everything that was happening, he found little time to think about it. Unfortunately, there seemed to be a serious problem to consider. Everyone just kept bouncing here and there, and at the moment it was dark and very wet. "Perhaps King Neptune," Sebastian called out, "you should tell us what an ocean is. I fear that we are experiencing a measure of discomfort, and because I do not understand what is happening I fear I am of little help."

King Neptune was well aware of the Starians' immediate confusion and concern, for like Ambassador Marius, he was one with the consciousness of all things. Therefore he sensed his young guests' concern over their current situation and began to carefully explain. "When you were together beneath the surface of your planet, the heat coming from your bodies pressed against the coldness of outer space. As you already know, this brought rains, which in turn, caused great floods. Eventually, the water gathered in the lower areas of your planet and became oceans, or large water masses.

"Water is actually comprised from various elements in the cosmos known as oxygen and hydrogen. Nonetheless, this ocean you now find yourself floating around in is not pure hydrogen and oxygen, because it is salty and salt includes other chemical compounds. In time, of course, you will find this salt quite satisfying to the taste.

"As it happens, my body is quite solid, for I am comprised of all four elements, earth, air, fire and water. I fear, however, that I consist more of hydrogen and oxygen, than those forms created for life on the solid landmasses. Your own bodies, of course, are hydrogen. As you build forms suitable for maneuvering in the sea, you will also have to take the necessary building material from the same elements or forces that I am comprised of."

King Neptune paused for a moment, wondering whether he should go on. He sensed the multitudinous questions lurking in the minds of all the Starians, but he decided that it would be better to let the subject of sea creation wait. He closed the subject, saying, "I believe that is enough explanation on this matter for the time being. Right now we really must get busy and work on your more immediate problem, that of creating some new bodies for you. Therefore, Sebastian, why don't you call your friends and we will begin."

Although there still remained many unanswered questions, Sebastian knew that questions only led to more questions, so he immediately signaled the other Starians to join him. Unfortunately, they had some difficulty in complying with his request, for every time King Neptune spoke the sea roared and the Starians were scattered here and there by the ocean waves.

By this time Jason, who was generally very quiet, became quite concerned and called out to the Lord of the Seas, "Sire, we still can't see you. We can hear your voice, but whenever you speak, the water becomes so turbulent that we lose our sense of direction. Besides, our bodies seem inclined to float, which is making things quite difficult."

"Look below you," King Neptune replied. "I am near a cave at the bottom of the sea."

From his habitat deep beneath the water's surface, the Ruler of the Sea shook his head, thinking, "Those sunlight bodies will indeed have to go. Otherwise, whenever I speak, my new students will be scattered all over the ocean."

While the Starians struggled to reach the classroom at the bottom of the sea King Neptune became silent in case he caused them more difficulty.

After a great deal of struggle, Sebastian and the others managed to arrive at the entrance of King Neptune's cave and, while they were not aware of it at the time, this cave would become their classroom throughout the fourth cosmic day of progression.

Immediately on their arrival Sebastian and the others were greeted with a most amazing sight. A very strange apparition peered down at them with kindly, but amused eyes. His hair was comprised of tangled seaweed, and while this was very intriguing, it was his body that captured most of the Starians' attention. King Neptune had a long tail, which they later learned, helped to propel him through the water. The upper part of him, however, resembled an earth human. On his head was golden crown of sunlight with seven points that had been given to him by Lord of the Stars to show that he was ruler of all the seas. These, of course, were not the only strange things Sebastian and the others saw, for the King's tail was forked at the end and brilliant green.

King Neptune tried to ignore the astonished looks of his new students, even though he was greatly entertained by them. However, this did not hinder him from starting with the necessary training the Starians needed. As soon as the undersea Ruler saw everyone lined up before him, he said, "It is probably obvious to you by now, that you are having difficulty maneuvering yourselves through the ocean. So, the very first thing you must do is to create new bodies more suitable for the sea. If you do not, we will accomplish very little."

Finally, having recovered somewhat from this first encounter with the ruler of the seas, Sebastian asked the question paramount on everyone's mind. "How can we create new bodies when we have been nothing but light since our birth?"

Looking beguilingly mysterious, King Neptune replied, "It is true that you are made of light, Sebastian, but that is only your outer reflection. You must always remember you are still an aspect of the Lord of the Stars, and he can create anything."

Webster, who actually enjoyed going up and down with the motion of the water, spoke up, "Does this mean that all one has to do is become very quiet and think? Ambassador Marius taught us that the Lord of the Stars built the Universe in this manner. First, the Lord conceived a perfect ideal, and then through perfect concentration, or will, the ideal slowly materialized into solid form."

"I remember being taught that," Sebastian chimed in, "And if that is so, then life on all planets must have begun exactly the same way. Perhaps if we just become quiet, our outer bodies would become what we think."

"Very good, Webster and Sebastian," replied King Neptune, "That is indeed the general idea. Now look closely at me, for the bodies you create should at least somewhat resemble mine, particularly my tail. The tail is very important, as it enables me to swim easily through the waves of the sea without being shaken around."

With these words, the Lord of the Seas swam smoothly through the waves, his tail making a gentle motion back and forth.

The Starians watched King Neptune maneuver with great interest. First he swam a short distance away from them and then he sailed toward the surface of the sea. Immediately he dove back down again. Next he curled his tail closely to his body, turned gracefully and returned. After he made a number of agile demonstrations to show his students the versatility of a fish body, he stopped in front of them.

Fascinated by what they had seen the Starians decided that to be like their teacher would certainly allow them a wonderful adventure. The idea of swimming everywhere, their tails creating perfect motion in the waves of the ocean, seemed almost as wonderful to everyone as the excitement they incurred when they were created and lived in the solar nebulae.

Seeing that his students had accepted the idea of new forms, King Neptune indicated that it was now time for the Starians to become silent. With the exception of the waves lapping back and forth, creating a soft kind of steady roar, all of Htrae became hushed. Time passed. Gradually, each Starian began to change into something different. Sebastian put on a silver suit, while Sally developed spots, and Cedric dressed in colorful stripes.

King Neptune was very pleased with the progress of his students and found it interesting to watch everyone build his or her own form according to their individual sense of purpose.

When, at last, each one of the Starians had completed their new forms sufficiently to learn at this particular level of development, it was time for them to take swimming lessons. Complete mastery over their present forms would enable them to move easily through the sea, and when this was accomplished, they would be ready for some of the more serious lessons of creation.

One day, after a number of decades had elapsed, King Neptune asked Cedric how he really felt about his new life. Cedric replied, "I know I am still who I am, even though my outer form has changed. Yet, sometimes I do have to work hard to remember that I am still actually what I was when we left our home in the Sun and not actually a fish at all. I also have to remember that it merely appears that I have created this new form, because I know that it is really the spirit of the Lord of the Stars within me that has made this possible."

The King beamed, for Cedric had answered the question exactly as he had hoped he would. Next he turned to Franklin. "Do you have anything to add to this, Franklin?"

For a few moments Franklin was silent, thinking very deeply. Finally he answered King Neptune's question, saying, "While I know that I am Starian, I also know that this new body has been necessary. Otherwise, it would not be possible for me to become life in the sea."

"This must mean that building a planet is done a step at a time." Sebastian interjected. "And, if this is true, who knows what kind of exciting forms we may need to build in the future!"

King Neptune nodded his head, realizing that his students were learning their lessons well. At the same time, he also knew that those who were more advanced would soon venture out of the sea.

One day, a rather amazing thing happened to Sebastian, who had been swimming further and higher each day. Suddenly he broke through the surface of the sea. Looking around, he was astonished to see how light it was. The shining waves almost hurt his eyes in spite of his glasses. At first Sebastian thought that he must have returned to his old Sun home high in the sky. He looked up. When he did so, he saw something very beautiful. Above him, the cosmos had taken on a beautiful blue color, and right in the middle of its vast blue expanse he saw the sun. He waved excitedly. Unfortunately, much to his dismay, he discovered that he was unable to remain on the surface of the sea any longer. As he turned, Sebastian realized that he had become too accustomed to breathing under water. Although he made several attempts to remain longer on the surface he could not do so and, exhausted, he returned to King Neptune's classroom.

As Sebastian swam downward, Ambassador Marius and the Lord of the Stars were having a chance meeting to discuss an inter-stellar war going on in one of the galaxies. Abruptly, in the middle of their conversation, the Ambassador smiled. "My Lord, I believe I just saw something move in one of the oceans on Htrae. It looked like Sebastian, although I fear he appears rather different now. He seems to be a fish."

The Lord of the Stars remained quiet for a brief time before answering, because it was necessary for him to first check that part of himself which lived in other things to make certain that there were no mistakes. He soon responded to Brother Marius' statement, saying, with a measure of obvious amusement, "Ambassador Marius, you are quite right. That tail you saw flashing on the surface of the water certainly did belong to Sebastian. You will have to admit, of course, that he is really rather handsome in his silver coat. And, I see that he is still curious as ever. He is even wearing those big square glasses you gave him."

Staring down at Htrae's ocean with a measure of curiosity, the Lord of the Stars added, "My, oh my, I do not believe I have ever seen a fish with glasses before."

"You are absolutely right, my Lord. Sebastian is really quite a remarkable sight," the Ambassador replied. "You know, I will have to start giving some special attention to Sebastian now, for it will be up to him to lead the others to their planet's surface. I'm looking forward, not only to working more extensively with Sebastian, but also to the time when all of the Starians will become human. Then *Operation Earth Angel* can really get underway. And when it does, I am confident that it will be a very exciting adventure for everyone."

Once they had finished discussing the matter of Htrae, the Lord of the Stars and Ambassador Marius returned to the pressing situation of the inter-stellar war. It was a well-known fact that whenever any two factions released a hydrogen bomb, the aftermath left a flow of disturbing ripples throughout the entire universe. Ambassador Marius certainly wanted to circumvent this from happening again if possible.

By this time Sebastian had arrived at the bottom of the sea. He was jubilant. "Come, everyone!" he cried, "Let me show you what I discovered today! I saw the Sun nebulae again. Please come and see!"

As the Starians followed Sebastian to the surface of the sea, King Neptune knew that the fifth cosmic day of progression was about to begin. Of course, his work would continue in the sea as long as the planet needed to support life. He well knew that new life would continue to come into being, progress and one day graduate. Because of this, the King was also very much aware that he was an integral link in the great cosmic plan.

Each day Sebastian continued to swim to the surface of the

sea. Some of the other Starian fish were too weak to follow and went back to their familiar habit of living at the bottom of the sea. There were others who did not believe that there was any end of the sea and they remained behind too. However, when Sebastian surfaced, for what would be one of the last times, his old friends Webster, Jason, Joan, Sally, Cedric and Franklin all surfaced with him.

After playing hide-n-seek in the waves for a time and waving their tails at the sun, Sebastian and the others tiredly returned to the schoolroom of King Neptune. With a measure of sadness they realized that their current forms were no longer adequate and they needed new bodies, ones that would allow them to live longer on top of the sea.

Once again, the Starians began to work on new forms. For those who did not reach the surface of the sea because they had not practiced their swimming daily, another time would come. Of course, their progression would be slower, but could not be halted. Fortunately, progression was a natural process of cosmic order.

As the sun set, the Lord of the Stars burst forth in the splendor of his night robe, signaling the end of the fourth cosmic period of Htrae's advancement. Tenderly, he took care of the great cosmic sea within him, ensuring that higher evolution was possible on all planets when it was earned. He was especially proud of those planets which had evolved so high that they became divine. These fulfilled his Great Plan and the life forms on these planets became his emissaries, helping other planets to grow and others to graduate.

As the Lord of the stars bid the Starians goodnight he also looked tenderly upon Earth, and he spoke to them through the consciousness of the unspoken word, "Soon, little Earth," he said, "You shall have your peace. Wait and see."

CHAPTER V

Creating Outer Forms

It took several centuries for the Starians to create an outer form suitable for life on the surface of their planet. Sometimes their experiments failed and their life forms did not conform to planetary conditions. It then became necessary to try again. Htrae was not the first planet in the one hundred and fifty billion known galaxies to face such difficulties. The same thing happened again and again on other planets throughout the universe and many species became extinct. This occurred because some environments failed to produce the preconditions necessary for a particular type of physical expression. When the preconditions for a particular expression or a species ceased, so did its life form.

Fortunately, souls never cease to exist, for they are a divine aspect of Lord of the Stars, and thus, immortal. When any physical expression does end, however, it becomes necessary for the indwelling soul to go through the painful process of adapting to a new outer form, one that will enable it to continue progression in its existing environment. For this reason, it was not particularly unusual to find that the Starians experienced the same struggles for survival as their planetary brothers and sisters had before them.

From fish bodies into reptiles, the Starians continued in their efforts to create forms that could survive on land. Finally Sebastian had, what he thought was a great idea. He decided to think a big thought, one that would create something large enough to live on the attractive landmass that he and the others had observed for so long.

Of course the more advanced Starians wanted to join Sebastian in the great *think fest*. Before they did, however, Sebastian decided that it would be important to instruct them concerning the matter of a proper prototype, or master plan. "First," he said, "we need long necks so we can see over the grass. Also, we must have something that will enable us to move across the land, as well as a powerful tail to propel us out of the sea."

When Sebastian saw that everyone was looking at him with a measure of anticipation, he said, "if you are ready, we will begin."

In view of the exciting possibility of walking on land, everyone waved his or her fish tail eagerly.

Thus, during the dawn of the fifth cosmic day of creation, from an observation point high in the heavens, Ambassador Marius observed a rather unusual sight. In the gleaming waters of the crystal planet, huge hulks rose from the sea. He shook his head in great astonishment and smilingly thought, "It appears that Sebastian got carried away with his thinking."

Ambassador Marius was not the only one to notice the strange phenomena occurring on Htrae's surface, for the Lord of the Stars was aware of it also. Although it was highly entertaining, the Lord had seen this same thing happen many times in other solar systems. It seemed that big ideas often produced big results, but unfortunately big results were not always practical. In spite of this, the Lord made it a practice to never interfere with planetary evolution. He had designed the universe in such a way as to assure that every soul progressed on its own merits and he knew that mistakes were good lessons for the soul. Now, as he saw the great Starian hulks moved toward land, he shook his head and forthwith sent Ambassador Marius a message. "Do not be overly concerned Ambassador. Mother Htrae will soon straighten them out."

As the massive forms rose from the sea, the land trembled wildly. Mother of Htrae, considered matriarch of Vegetation, was in deep contemplation. She looked up startled. On seeing the great hulks moving toward her, she became immediately concerned, although she had been working for a long time with the Starian essence emanating through the surface of the sea and knew every Starian by name.

While she had waited for the Htrae family, Mother Htrae kept herself very busy. She had to prepare many things to insure the survival of all life forms that would eventually occupy the planet. This included creating grasses, herbs, trees, flowers, vegetables and fruit. Now the Starians had finally arrived, and she could do little but stare at them in amazement. Even as they walked, their massive bodies rattled the entire planet with every step. As Mother Htrae felt the ground shake beneath her feet, she shook her head in much the same way Ambassador Marius had when he first viewed the new Starian forms. "Much work will be needed on those bodies," she thought. "If they remain this way, they will create major disasters all over the planet."

"Good morning, my little Starians," Mother Htrae said when she was finally able to speak. For a moment, however, she did have to pause and reconsider the word "little" before continuing. "Please allow me to introduce myself. I am Mother Htrae, your new teacher. My major responsibilities will be to help you prepare for human bodies."

The Starians' new teacher allowed her eyes to sweep over each member of the family carefully in order to itemize everything they would need. "Let's see," she said, almost under her breath, "There is food to eat, water to drink, air and sunlight."

Then, speaking louder, Mother Htrae added, "I greatly fear that you will eventually have to do something about your life forms if you are to continue life on this planet. They are much too large."

On hearing these words the Starians looked at the mother of vegetation with doleful eyes. They had tried very hard and actually thought that they had done quite well.

When Mother Htrae realized that her words had deeply affected her new students, her gaze became gentler. She knew that the appearance of the Starians meant that life on land could really begin and this was a prerequisite for people bodies. It would be her mission to see that these kindly creatures were fed during their days on land and, in turn, obedience to her ways would ensure that they would never become ill.

The Starians were just as startled over the appearance of their new teacher as she had been of them. They looked her over with intense curiosity. She wore a dress of brown dirt and had masses of green grass growing out of her head. As if that was not sufficiently astounding; sitting on top of her green hair was a large bonnet made of various fruits, while her skirt contained different kinds of vegetables.

This time it was Sally who recovered first. She sought to be very polite, just as she had been taught in the solar classroom. When she tried to curtsy, however, her foot sank into the sand and she got stuck. It took Franklin and Jason a few moments to get her out, and then even more time elapsed before Sally overcame her embarrassment. Finally, she stammered, "Gree-ee-tings, Mother Htrae. We are tr-u-u-ly happy to meet you. We have been working a very long time in an effort to develop forms that would enable us to live on land and we had almost given up."

"My! My! It is nice to meet you also, Sally," the mother of Htrae replied. "Certainly I have been aware of the difficulties you incurred while creating your present forms. Of course it is quite obvious that you and the others must have had a very big thought in order to create such massive life bodies. Nonetheless, they will have to suffice for the time being, although you will ultimately find that they are too bulky for comfort. Also, your current life forms will require a great deal of food and they make a terrible noise when you walk around. Nothing on the planet will be able to sleep!"

"I must admit that these hulks are far more difficult to move around in than our fish bodies were," agreed Sebastian. "But if I keep thinking, I am afraid I will keep growing larger forms. I dare venture that is not the solution."

Mother Htrae's eyes twinkled merrily. "Perhaps Sebastian instead of thinking big, as you have done since the beginning of your planet's creation, you should think smaller. Always remember that the power within you is really infinite and is only limited by your thoughts. It is up to you."

"Of course," Sebastian almost shouted in his excitement. "Why didn't I think of that a long time ago?"

Mother Htrae simply smiled and said, "You did not think of it because you became accustomed to thinking only large thoughts. You will learn one day that in doing the same thing all the time you create limitations."

"What do you mean, we will create limitations?" asked Webster.

"Its' rather difficult to explain Webster," Mother Htrae replied, "but doing the same thing all the time builds a wall. This wall is invisible, but nonetheless real, and often what one builds one has a great deal of trouble escaping."

"I don't understand," said Webster. "If the wall is invisible, then how can it have any affect?"

"Lets see if I can explain it another way," Mother Htrae answered. Say, you thought about the same thing every day, like eating the fruit at the top of that tree over there. If you kept eating it every day, one day there would not be any more fruit at the top. Because you wouldn't know that plant life beneath the tree could be eaten also you could easily starve to death. Thus, eating that fruit at the top of the tree, and only that fruit, will become a limitation. Do you understand?"

"I think so," Webster replied.

"Don't worry about it Webster, you will understand soon enough. You see, those massive hulks of your new life forms will teach you about limitation soon enough," Mother Htrae smiled. "Now come, everyone. Let me introduce you to the planet you have helped to build. You must remember, however, there is still a long way to go and many things to learn before you can actually begin *Operation Earth Angel.*"

As they walked along in the cool green forest toward their next classroom, Jason felt such great happiness he began to sing. Terrible sounds emanated from him in the form of high squawks and low gawks. Mother Htrae looked behind her. There had never been such unpleasant noises since the beginning of Htrae. She had listened to thunder when it rained and the rumblings of the Starians when they stretched under the land. She had heard the wind blow and the slap of the ocean, but those sounds had been natural and beautiful. What she now heard coming from Jason was raucous and disturbing.

"Jason, what ever are you doing?" Mother Htrae inquired — her tone a bit stern.

"Why, I am singing," Jason, replied. "This land is very lovely and it feels so good to be able to walk, to see the sun, and to be free. Besides, such a beautiful planet must be honored with glorious music."

Mother Htrae grew silent when she heard Jason's answer. She did not wish to hurt his feelings, or discourage him, but his singing was disturbing every one. Before she could speak again, however, the Lord of the Stars revealed Jason's mission on Htrae to her. The Queen saw that he would become a great composer one day and bring wondrous music to those who lived on his planet. Thus, when she spoke again she was gentle and very solemn.

"You are quite right, of course, Jason. Htrae does need music. Unfortunately, at this moment, I fear yours leaves much to be desired. I suggest that you consider practicing a bit. Listen to the wind in the forest, the waves upon the sea, and the sounds of all living things. Stop to smell the flowers, see the splendor of the sunsets, and then try to imitate them in your music. I am confident it will sound much better then."

On hearing Mother Htrae's advice, everyone laughed, even though they did not want Jason to feel badly.

As they followed their new teacher, the Starians soon found themselves going deeper and deeper into the forest. Because of their size they made a great deal of noise as they pushed their way through the thick underbrush. Sometimes the earth seemed to shake beneath their feet, and when they tried to talk their voices were even more amazing. The words sounded more like roars, screeches and squawks. Still, each Starian seemed to know what the other was saying, although at the moment King Neptune and their sun home seemed far away.

Suddenly, those who were walking in front heard a terrible commotion behind them. There was a loud squawk, a roar, the earth began to shake, and a giant rustling filled the air. Turning to see what the problem was, they were met with a most remarkable sight. Apparently Cedric had gotten himself caught between two trees and couldn't get through. They saw that a tree pinning him down on each side of his large stomach. His front half had successfully maneuvered the narrow space, but his rear part was swaying back and forth as he tugged and pulled. Even though the Starian was digging his feet into the earth in an effort to push himself through, he was obviously making no headway.

Immediately the group returned to where Cedric was stuck in order to help him. At first they just stood there staring at him with amazement. Finally Mother Htrae walked around him to see if there was simple solution to Cedric's predicament. She did not wish to destroy any of the trees if possible.

"Cedric, how in the world did you get into this situation? Surely you did not think that the space between these two trees was large enough to allow you to pass through them?"

"The problem, Mother Htrae, is that I didn't think," Cedric replied. "I forgot I was in this big body and that I was not a fish. Anyway, I promise I will be more careful in the future, that is if I ever get out of here."

By this time Sebastian had sized up the situation and reached a possible solution. "I have an idea that might work," he said. "Our bodies are as big as his. Therefore, if we gather some strong vines and wrap them around each tree and pull, we might be able to pull the trees further apart. They appear quite flexible. Sally, Franklin and Jason, you can pull on one tree, while Joan, Webster and I pull on the other."

For the next few minutes the group was busy searching for flexible, but very strong, vines. Whenever they found one, they chewed it off with their teeth. After they had gathered several they returned to Cedric who had finally ceased thrashing around. They found that it was quite difficult to get the vines around the tree because they had to do it with their mouths. Finally, however, after several attempts, they succeeded. As they paused to puff and pant they began thinking that their new forms were really not very practical. Besides, they were very hungry. It was obvious, however, that for the time being they would have to put these problems behind them and focus on helping their friend. They divided into two teams and got on each side and began to pull, squawking, screeching and roaring the entire time. Their first try did not work.

It was Mother Htrae who first realized why the rescue attempt had failed. She said to Cedric, "Cedric, you can't just stand there, you have to draw your breath in so that your stomach will be smaller. At the same time you are going to have to push yourself forward. I know it isn't easy, but you can do it."

Cedric nodded his head and drew his breath in. He could see that Mother Htrae's suggestion was helpful, although he knew that drawing in his breath alone would not be sufficient get free. He still needed some assistance.

Once again the teams got on each side of him and as they pulled, Cedric drew his breath in and pushed. Suddenly he found himself going headfirst into the tree in front of him. This proved to be quite painful, and for a moment his head was filled with stars. Nevertheless, he was free from his entrapment. The rest of the Starians breathed a sigh of relief, although it was obvious that there was still another problem. At the moment Cedric was in a kneeling position and they had to get him up on his feet. So they gathered around him again, and with a measure of huffs and puffs, thrashing and the usual loud dinosaur rumbles, Cedric was finally upright.

With another sigh of relief, everyone formed a line behind their Htraeon Mother and continued toward their new classroom in the Forest, their great hulks swaying from side-to-side. When they had finally settled down from their recent ordeals, Mother Htrae began the first lesson.

"You must never take more from the land than you need," she cautioned. "If you do, you will develop greed and become afraid of having less. Our Lord of the Stars will never produce more Starians than there is food for. His way is perfect and he makes no mistakes."

"How come people on human planets are hungry then?" asked Franklin.

"Because they do not always share with each other," Mother

Htrae replied. "People have built great cities and established money systems. Even though their reason was to establish an outer form of cosmic distribution to make certain that each person got what they worked for, the system was also flawed. It bred jealousy, anger, hatred, war and death, for those who still did not always work tried to take what they wanted through violence. If each soul always helped those less fortunate, however, the perfect law of our Lord of the Stars would be fulfilled. Because they do not, the poor soon become diseased and the rich become afraid of losing their wealth. They simply forget that sharing with their neighbors really means helping everyone on the planet.

"You see, when someone only helps his or her immediate neighbor, he or she limits the size of the world to that community. On the other hand, when someone decides to help everyone on his or her planet, that person's world expands until it is as large as the planet. There is a great deal of difference."

Sebastian was, as usual, bubbling with excitement. "It must be somewhat like growing bodies," he exclaimed. "If someone loves only one's own family, then they live in a very small world and their love will be only as big as that small world. But if someone seeks to love everyone in the world, then that love becomes as big as his or her world. And that would be very large indeed. Certainly that explains why Lord of the Stars is so great; he loves everyone and everything in the universe."

Sebastian paused for a moment and then added, "I guess he must be larger than even the universe."

"Very good, Sebastian," Mother Htrae said smiling. "That is the key to building a harmonious planet. Many planets have not yet learned that sharing with one's neighbor means sharing with everyone on the planet and loving all life equally. Help is not just giving; it is also living as a reflection of the Lord of the Stars, the source of all life. It means mutual respect for every soul who is part of a solar system, or even a part the universe."

"Will those who do not know these things ever discover the teachings of the Lord of the Stars in time to save their planets?" Sally asked.

"Let us hope so, Sally," Mother Htrae answered quietly.

When class was concluded, the Starians made their way back into the forest. Each was thinking about the things that Mother Htrae had discussed. They vowed that they would love everything, including every star, in order to become more like the Lord of the Stars. By this time, they also realized that they had another problem they needed to take care of, and that was to create smaller bodies. Helping Sally when she curtseyed and getting Cedric out of the trees, as well as the fact that they were hungry all the time had proven to them that their dinosaur bodies were absolutely too massive.

Once again Sebastian gathered the family together, this time under the great trees of the forest. His purpose was to discuss the subject of creating new forms.

By day the deep blue sky and the sun looked down on the Starians, and by night the stars lit up the night sky. Many centuries of Earth time passed before the Starians were able to produce forms without long necks and huge bodies. These new forms were much more comfortable, and the back pains which the family had always suffered went away. Of course, large creatures still came to live for a short time on the planet, for the weaker Starians who had not made it out of the sea the first time finally did so. It was natural that they duplicated all of the things that the first Starians had done, but their discomfort did not last as long. Not only did they experience Mother Htrae's wonderful teachings, but they also had the senior Starians to help them. Thus, their progression was faster. Because of this, each still remembered their origin and peace continued to reign across Htrae.

In spite of the Starians' ability to work together harmoniously, the most dangerous period of their progression still lay ahead of them. It would not be long before they would develop people bodies, and with this came reasoning power and free choice.

Before much more time elapsed the dinosaurs of Htrae became extinct, and eventually different life forms occupied the jungles and in the sea. Some of the bodies which the Starians created proved to be almost as impractical as the great hulks. Either they were unable to reach the succulent fruit in the top of the trees, or if they could, they were unable to live well on the surface of the planet. Sometimes, the family just looked at each other and laughed, for some of the forms were most unusual. Perhaps the most ridiculous was the spotted camcalf, which seemed to be part camel and part cow. The form might have worked, if Webster had not designed two of the legs to point frontward and the other two to go in the opposite direction. These not only caused great merriment among the senior members of Htrae, but also caused them study their planet more closely in order to create bodies that could be sustained by the environment.

In spite of the kaleidoscope of forms which the Starians created, it was always easy to locate them. One reason was Sebastian. He remained extraordinarily curious, and because of this he had never parted with his glasses. From his dinosaur body, throughout his creation of numerous forms, his big square glasses always bobbed up and down on his nose. Of course, he was not the only one to possess such a peculiarity. Webster had a pen growing from the center of his head, while Cedric had a paintbrush. Jason had some kind of a kind of musical note and Franklin had a light bulb which kept going on and off. The girls had been included of course; Joan had been assigned a cross and Sally wore a hair ribbon. This phenomenon had occurred, because the Lord of the Stars had created each Starian for a special purpose and he did not want them to forget what their purpose was. Therefore, no matter where the Htrae family went their particular mission was always within them, or perhaps better described, as being on top of their heads.

As the Starians ventured further and further from the forest to seek new homes, they found some caves in a mountain. They discovered that by living in these they were cooler in the summer and warmer in the winter. The caves also offered greater protection from the storms, and so little by little Sebastian and the others set up a community within the caves. Because the Starians were so busy, they little realized they were now only a few Earth years away from birth into people bodies.

One day, while they were in their forest classroom, Mother Htrae said, "You must always remember that everyone is equal and no one is any more special than someone else. Although environment and climate often affect the advancement of life forms, one's progression is determined by their ability to work in harmony with the universal plan created by the Lord of the Stars. Therefore, every soul must pass through each phase of Soul progression just as you have. Even those who often seem less advanced, or evolved, will evolve and become great some day. In order to develop the inherent tendencies of heaven you must help those who are less fortunate than yourselves, for it is a basic law of progression.

"Before long you will be leaving your forest home to become human. Before you go, I want to tell you that you have all done very well, and I believe you will indeed be a remarkable people. Sadly, I fear that I must remain behind to teach the next insurgence of Starians."

"Oh! Mother Htrae," Sally cried, "We will miss you terribly, but I know that we must not be selfish and that you are needed by others. Nonetheless, we will remember you whenever we see beautiful flowers, wonderful fruit and great trees."

"I agree with Sally, we will truly miss you Mother Htrae" added Sebastian, "yet, I am beginning to feel an urgency to move on and this is exciting. It is almost as though we cannot progress any further in these life forms. Why, we have been looking forward to people bodies ever since we were created."

In the far distant regions of space, the Lord of the Stars and Ambassador Marius beamed with joy when the fifth cosmic epoch neared its end. Never had the sunset been more colorful or the skies bluer, as the first faint glimmer of all the evening stars appeared. The whole galaxy was excited as the sapphire planet prepared to give birth to human form, for the entire solar system would also then advance. This meant that all solar systems in all galaxies would also become greater.

CHAPTER VI

Science of Sir Cellular

As the sun rose on the morning of the sixth cosmic day, Sebastian opened his eyes and stretched. He felt different: quite light and almost the same as when he lived in the sun without form. He looked down at his body, and what he saw caused him great alarm. He was no longer covered with hair! His body was thin-skinned and almost transparent. Immediately he became concerned. When he looked around the cave he saw that the other Starians had changed also. Fearing that some terrible disease had befallen them, Sebastian decided that he had better contact Ambassador Marius.

As Sebastian rushed out of the cave he could not help but appreciate the agility of this new form, for he could move more quickly now. However, the rocks hurt his feet and he had to stop to wrap them in thick leaves to cushion his walking.

When he had finally walked a short distance from the cave Sebastian looked around with a measure of confusion. For some reason things looked different. The trees seemed taller, the flowers appeared brighter, and even though he was still wearing his big square glasses, the sun hurt his eyes. Closing his eyes and mustering up all of his thought force, Sebastian cried, "Ambassador Marius, you must come at once. Something terrible has happened to us."

Immediately a shadow fell across the path in front of Sebastian. He looked up to see Ambassador Marius standing before him. As usual, the Ambassador seemed to appear from nowhere — a fear that always amazed the Starians. It had not seemed so, however, when they lived in the sun and everyone was light. Now, all of this had changed. During the recent centuries, Ambassador Marius had found it necessary to appear to Sebastian and the others in a more solid form, for their eyes were no longer acclimated to seeing things of higher vibratory frequencies.

"Why, Sebastian, what is the problem?" asked Ambassador Marius.

"Look at me, Ambassador, something terrible has happened," Sebastian cried. "The rocks hurt my feet and I can almost see through myself and, worse, Sally, Jason and the others appear the same way. It seems that we may have contracted some terrible disease."

As he heard Sebastian spewing out his concern, Ambassador Marius found it somewhat difficult to contain his amusement. Obviously the cause of all this confusion was Sebastian's people body. When he could sufficiently contain the inclination to chuckle openly, Ambassador Marius explained, "There is really no problem, Sebastian. You have simply become human. You, Jason, Cedric and all of the others have been waiting a very long time for this and must have asked me numerous times when it would happen. Now look at you, you're really quite handsome, you know; certainly more so than some of the forms you have dreamed up in the past."

The Ambassador paused a moment and then shook his head, "Nonetheless, Sebastian, you must realize that these bodies will require special training. Therefore, it is time for me to introduce you to another new teacher."

Sebastian was a bit concerned, because he really did not wish Ambassador Marius to leave so quickly. At the same time, he looked forward to learning more about this strange world he and the other Starians had just entered.

Before the Ambassador departed, he said, "Remember Sebastian, make room in your heart for all of your teachers. Planets are very big and solar systems even larger, which means that no one person can contain all of the truth. As soon as you begin to accept what only one teacher teaches, you may limit yourself and begin to believe that all other teachers are wrong. This might cause disagreements, much like those existing on other people planets.

"Now," Ambassador Marius smiled, "Don't you think it is time for us to call the others together and explain the situation? Besides, it is time to introduce you to Sir Cellular, the ruler of all cell life."

When the other Starians had assembled Ambassador Marius explained the nature of their people bodies, and then he summoned a most unusual teacher. Immediately an amazing sight met everyone's eyes, for the new arrival was almost completely transparent and had millions of little circles moving inside of an almost liquefied body. Ambassador Marius then introduced him, "This is Sir Cellular. He will teach you all about your new bodies and how to take care of them. I venture that you will find his instruction quite fascinating, particularly you Sebastian, for you will be entering the scientific world of cell life."

As always the Ambassador quickly dematerialized, leaving the

Starians extraordinarily curious over the mention of cell life. They did not have to ponder on the matter long, for their attention was almost immediately pulled back to Sir Cellular. He smiled down at them and said, "While I may be new to you, I am really very old; for I have taught on all planets where human form has appeared. Even though I am the ruler of cell life, I am still governed by our Lord of the Stars who causes even the tiniest cell to live and function. Therefore, it is very important to care for your body.

"The body is a remarkable thing and is actually made out of the same material that the universe is. Perhaps another way to think of it is to realize that your bodies are made of stardust and that they draw nourishment from the universe. When the body is subjected to things that are not natural, such as those things that are not provided for by planetary production, it succumbs to disease and illness."

"Is that what some of the people on people planets have done?" asked Joan in a somewhat quiet voice.

"Yes, Joan, it is," Sir Cellular replied. "However, I do not wish any of you to feel too badly about this, because numerous planets passing from animal life have made the same mistake. Unfortunately, illness, old age and death slow down the progression of the soul. This would not be so serious, if it were not that sick people are unable help take proper care of themselves or their planet. As you well know from your own progression, when the pre-conditions to sustain a certain life form cease to prevail, that life form must terminate. Remember when you were dinosaurs?

At the mention of dinosaurs, the Starians laughed and nodded their heads up and down vigorously.

Of course Sebastian had a question, "But if soul progression is the purpose, then isn't it best done by keeping one's mind upon the Lord of the Stars and fulfilling one's purpose?"

"Now that depends on what a person's concept of progression is," responded Sir Cellular. "It is really difficult to give attention to either the Lord of the Stars, or one's purpose, when the body is ill. Therefore, care of the human body is an integral part of the soul's responsibility. If an illness consumes the body and it is not stopped, then the body may cease to exist. In turn, if the lessons that must be learned through human, or people forms, are not learned, the process of graduating from human to divine is slowed down."

Although Sir Cellular could see that the Starians had many questions, he felt that they should take some time and get used to their new people bodies, so he said, "That is probably enough for the moment."

Seeing the disappointment on his new student's faces, Sir Cellular added, "Don't worry, we will be seeing a lot of each other in the days ahead. I am confident that all of your questions will be answered in due time. However, at the moment I believe you need to take some time and get to know your people bodies. You will find them quite different than anything you have experienced so far."

For the next few days the Starians spent their time becoming used to their people bodies. They liked how light they felt and they liked the ease with which they could move around. At the same time, they also found that the bodies could be injured more easily than some of their other life forms, and their people forms were certainly not as warm as others had been. The Starians were pleased, however, that their new bodies did not have the thickness of the dinosaur skin, the rough scaled hide of the alligator, or the furry coat they had worn when they lived as orangutans. At the same time Sebastian, Joan, and all the others were also happy because they would soon be able to start their mission.

One day, when they had gathered in their earth classroom, Joan asked Sir Cellular, "What will happen to all the souls on Earth and all the Starians on Htrae when they become divine?"

"You will learn the answer to your question sometime in the near future Joan," replied Sir Cellular, looking very mysterious. "But first you must learn to take care of your bodies." With this Sir Cellular reached into his body and pulled out a handful of cells.

"See these?" he continued. "They are cells which I have removed from my body so that you can study them better. First you will notice that each cell is really quite independent when separated from the body."

Franklin, seeing how easy it was, immediately tried to reach into his body and get a handful of cells. He was unable to do so, and asked, "Sir Cellular, why can you do that and I cannot?" he asked.

Sir Cellular looked at Franklin with amusement, "Because I am vibrating at a different ratio than you are. This means the cells in my body are moving more rapidly. In fact, if they were moving much faster, I would be invisible to you. You would then be unable to see me at all."

"That must be why no one can see Lord of the Stars. He must be vibrating so fast that he is invisible to everyone," Sebastian added.

"That is not quite true, Sebastian, the Lord of the Stars is really pure consciousness and therefore invisible, but he does express through all things visible. Therefore he is the primary cause of all motion. I greatly fear it would be very difficult to be exactly like him. See, even I have a form. Now look at yourself and see your body as it really is rather than what it appears to be. When I wave my hand, something unusual will happen to you." He did so and, in a flash, Sebastian's body turned into a very remarkable spectacle.

"Why, I am almost all water!" Sebastian declared. "The cells are really like islands in a great sea."

"That is quite right, Sebastian," Sir Cellular replied. "The human body is primarily comprised of water and can be called the human ocean. From this ocean all people cells draw their food. This is similar to the way you lived when you were in the bottom of the sea with King Neptune."

Then, Jason, who had been studying the situation quite seriously, spoke up. "It seems that our bodies are just like the planets. They have oceans and great countries — if we call those things countries," he said pointing to Sebastian's heart and lungs.

"That is a good comparison, Jason. If you watch the movement of the cells closely, you will see that each country, or organ, actually vibrates at a different speed. Let us take a look at a drawing of Earth."

Sir Cellular began to draw a map of Earth, carefully putting all the different countries in it. "Look," he said, pointing to the map. "There is India, Africa, and the United States, yet life is truly a little different in each land. Even the various people bodies tend to be somewhat different, although everyone is actually part of the same planet."

"That's it! ... That's it!" Sally bubbled, jumping up and down excitedly. "Why, people on a planet are actually all one body and each planet is a cell in the cosmic body of Lord of the Stars, just like each one of these cells are all part of our own body."

Cedric chimed in; "It is obvious that everyone is much like a small solar system. Therefore, unity is actually a perfect state. It appears that all the secrets of the universe can be found in our new bodies."

"Well done ... well done," Sir Cellular responded, looking very pleased. Then he continued teaching. "Now when one of these cells dies, the work load increases for the others and soon the entire body becomes ill. The same thing can happen to a planet. When one person becomes ill, or fails to accept his role in planetary work, it weakens the entire planet."

"Wow! Look at Sebastian's heart!" cried Cedric. "When it beats it really stirs up everything in the human solar system."

"Quite right, Cedric, and if it were to stop beating, the entire human body would die. Of course, the soul, which contains the body, does not die."

"Then what happens to Starians if their body dies, but they do not?" Sebastian asked.

"You will learn that answer when you go to the Elsewhere Land, an unseen world where you live when you have worn out your body."

"What if we should have to go to this Elsewhere Land before our mission is complete?" Sally inquired.

"Well, Sally, then you would simply have to take another physical form. Now, perhaps you are beginning to see how important it is to have a healthy body. As we have discussed before, if you are careless with your body and you were to make too many visits to the Elsewhere Land, the soul evolution of all the Starians would be slowed down."

"The cells in our body are really like little people then, and their lives are really quite dependent upon us, aren't they?" Cedric asked.

"Yes, we can call them *Little People* if you like. In fact, it may help you to understand life in your new human bodies better," answered Sir Cellular. Then he added, "However, that is quite enough for today and class is dismissed. Tomorrow we will study more about this mysterious land of the Little People."

Pausing for a moment, Sir Cellular looked at Sebastian with considerable amusement. "I suppose I had better restore you to your solid self, Sebastian, or you will slosh around all day!" With this Sir Cellular raised his hand, and instantly Sebastian appeared very solid, although he knew that he really wasn't.

The Starians enjoyed school more than anything else, because learning assured the constant and upward climb of soul progression. Nonetheless, they also liked to play. They still had urges to swim in the beautiful crystal water, even though they could no longer stay under the water very long. In fact, it was as difficult for them to remain beneath the surface of the ocean as it had once been for them to stay on top.

Their biggest recreational adventure was trying to figure out a way to fly, for within everyone lives the desire to be free. When Sebastian and the others saw a soaring bird, it was hard not to want to fly, too. Eventually this inherent desire to ascend aloft got Franklin into various kinds of trouble, for he was always trying to create new methods to accomplish this feat.

One day Franklin picked up a number of large feathers off the ground which had been dropped by flying birds. He made great wings out of these by using red clay soil to hold the feathers together. Then he allowed them to dry in the sun. When the wings were completely dry, Franklin climbed a tree with them. He intended to soar out of the tree exactly like birds did. This was a disaster in the making, for the wings were so heavy that he immediately fell directly onto the hard ground, making a decidedly loud plopping noise when he landed. The wings were broken into hundreds of pieces and strewn all over the ground. When Franklin tried to stand up he discovered that his leg was injured, although it was apparently not broken. As he pulled himself up he thought, "I can see that these people bodies are actually something that may need repair from time to time."

In the meantime, Cedric, who had been sitting on the ground, began to draw this ridiculous and unfortunate flying spectacle onto a large, flat stone. He carefully drew Franklin with his wings against a big sun; little realizing that someone might come along in the future and think it was a drawing of some creature from outer space.

Later Sir Cellular explained these strange urges of the Starians, saying, "You must understand that the outer form is only partially responsible for soul progression. The inner part of you has a great deal to do with the things you like to do, or don't like to do. For instance, you like for swim, because once you dwelled beneath the sea. You like to fly, because once you flew above earth and dwelled in trees. Although you have now developed people bodies that will not let you do these things in the same manner you once did, there is still the tendency to want to do so."

"Therefore," the ruler of cell life taught; "the experiences of your past have a direct bearing on your experiences of today, while your purpose in life as created by the Lord of the Stars has a direct bearing on your future."

"Does this mean that we will continue to be motivated by the things of the past even as we fulfill our future?" asked Cedric.

"Something like that Cedric," Sir Cellular replied. "Your destiny has already been designed within you. In fact, it was designed before you ever existed, and in time each of you will become what you are supposed to be. Nothing can stop this, because you are all part of the Lord's plan for the universe. You see the *Great Plan* is like a thought. It was created and then becomes, thus constantly molding itself into what it was ultimately designed for. Therefore, all of the suns and their solar systems are moving forward in a rotating spiral, and are ever expanding as the Lord of the Stars fulfills his *Great Plan.* How long it will take you or any soul in a people body, to fulfill their individual purpose depends on one's ability to conform to the Plan. In the meantime it is natural for each of you to want to swim and fly, although you have already learned that these things cannot not be accomplished in the fashion they once were."

Later, the Starians discussed the matter of inherent tendencies and decided that these were not necessarily bad. They agreed that the past had helped them to become what they were today and that made each one unique. They also liked the idea of trying to find new ways to do things they had enjoyed in the past.

Every morning, the Htrae family rose early like Sir Cellular had instructed. They liked to watch the changing colors of dawn, for they had never forgotten their sun home, King Neptune, or Mother Htrae, even as they continued to learn new things. They were often reminded that their bodies were not only water, but also made up of sunlight and air, making it possible to utilize the basic elements of sun, water, air, and earth for healthier lives. As the Starians learned to work with these natural forces they seldom saw illness. However, if illness did overtake them because they participated in something unnatural to their people bodies, Sir Cellular taught them how draw from the forces of sun, water, air and earth to heal his or her self.

The ruler of cell life taught, "By now you know that your new people bodies are comprised of the four elements. Thus, in order to have a healthy life you must remain harmonious with the life forces around you, such as the sun, water, flowers and trees. Your bodies draw some of the nutrients from these forces naturally, because you are made out of the same elements and like attracts like."

"It is difficult for me to understand how that happens," Joan, who was often the quiet one, spoke up.

"I suppose it does sound rather complex Joan," Sir Cellular replied. "Let's see if I can make it simpler. Remember, you learned that everything is one. For this reason all things have a tendency to unite with its parent provider, such as the hydrogen and oxygen in your human ocean will attempt to replenish itself from the sun and the air.

"I see," Joan said, greatly intrigued. "If we expose our bodies to the sun, then the hydrogen in our human ocean will act somewhat like a magnate and attract the hydrogen of sun. This will restore what has been used."

"Not only will it restore, Joan, but it will also purify. When some part of your body becomes ill, you can increase the intensity of the forces with the power of your mind."

These words immediately heightened everyone's curiosity. Cedric immediately asked, "And how is that possible Sir Cellular?"

"Well Cedric, you already know that you managed to create your forms to adjust to the surrounding pre-conditions. Thus, it should not be too difficult to understand that by focusing your mind on, say the sun, you could increase the amount of solar particles you draw to you. And, if you breathe in as you focus on the sun, you will have even greater control over the incoming solar energy than you would otherwise. The solar particles have no individual minds, so they must surrender to your will. As you let your breath out, direct the sun's energy to any part of the body you wish, again with the power of the mind."

Sir Cellular paused for a moment thoughtfully. Then he said, "Perhaps some cloud zapping will help you to understand the power of the mind."

"What do mean, cloud zapping?" Franklin queried, trying to somewhat contain his constant curiosity.

Sir Cellular looked at Franklin with a measure of amusement. "Well, Franklin. You have been curious about splitting an atom. Why don't you start by splitting clouds?"

By this time everyone was looking at Sir Cellular in amazement. Splitting clouds, they wondered, how could anyone actually split a cloud?

Noting their amazement, as well as the questions on their mind, Sir Cellular continued. "It is really quite easy, but I suggest small puffy white clouds in the beginning. Unfortunately, the larger a cloud is the longer it takes to split it. All you have to do is to focus your consciousness on a cloud and perceive it dividing, but do not allow your mind be drawn away. Eventually the mindless cloud must surrender to your greater power and do what you will it to do."

"Remember," Sir Cellular cautioned, "this is really an experiment to help you understand the power of your mind. It is not to consume too much of your time. You have many other far more important things to do."

As soon as Sebastian and the others were released from the classroom, they hastened to a nearby grassy knoll. Laying down flat on their backs, they each began to focus on a cloud. Within a few minutes seven white clouds became fourteen smaller clouds. This naturally led to speculation about halting storms and calming seas. Later, however, when Webster tried to zap a huge black thunderhead, he found that his mind was not yet developed sufficiently to do so. Somewhat chagrined, he reached the conclusion, that stilling the winds and calming the seas would have to wait until he and the others were much more advanced than they were at the moment.

In spite of a setback here or there, the Htrae family was intent on following Sir Cellular's instruction in all matters. On rising, they drank plenty of water and bathed. After this they ate a healthy breakfast comprised of fresh berries or some other fruit, and when breakfast was finished they usually returned to their schoolroom. This seemed quite natural to them, for Sebastian and the others had been in one school or another ever since they had been created, as had all of the other planets in the vast universe. For this reason, the Starians accepted the fact that this was what life was all about, a constant progression from one's current level of progression to the next. They liked becoming more and found that progression was fun. Because of this, they tried to carefully master every task placed before them, knowing that each new level opened the doorway to greater powers and a more advanced role in co-creation.

One day in the forest classroom, when everyone was looking closely at some of Sir Cellular's cells, Webster saw little rays of light coming from them and asked the teacher what they were.

"Webster, the rays of light coming out of the cells are somewhat like antennae. They transmit and receive impressions. Therefore, each one of these little cell-people living in your body not only eats what you eat, but also receives your thoughts," answered Sir Cellular.

"Then if we were to dislike our bodies because they are fat, or thin, or because we think they are ugly, we would be unkind to all the little sell-people and they would not remain healthy, would they?" Webster asked.

"Indeed not, Webster. Because of this we must be careful about what we eat and what we think. Those little antennae-like beams also draw oxygen, solar energy, and water to replace what is used daily to sustain the life of your people bodies. If you don't drink enough water or get enough sunshine, soon the little people inside will die and subsequently the body will die, too. Just as there are certain things the little sell-people need, there are some things they cannot abide, such as unclean air, unclean food, and unclean drink. When the oceans of the body become polluted and stop the little dwellers from living in their natural environment, they also suffer and die."

"Tell us more about that," Cedric requested, for he was becoming very interested in the biochemistry of his new body.

"Well, Cedric, you must remember that you have been developing bodies to suit your outer surroundings for thousands of years," Sir Cellular replied.

"That is true, but so have all of the others," Cedric interjected.

"Of course," Sir Cellular acknowledged. "For millions of years your little cell-people have lived on plant life, water, air and sun. These are elements and the natural food of the cells. As your fish bodies ate seaweed and dined on salt water, the cells formed to give you a body which would live in those conditions."

"Of course, now I am beginning to understand," Sebastian reflected. "That is why it took so long to build people bodies. The little people could only grow more advanced bodies as our real selves advanced."

"Naturally," Sir Cellular applauded. "Now you are getting the idea. When you eat and drink poorly, the little people are cut off from the natural way they have lived for thousands of years. They cannot exist without the very things they are made of. Each unnatural element they take into their bodies makes it more difficult for them to breathe. You might say they are like a great city, which has been cut off from the source of its supplies. Without fresh supplies going into the cell cities, people bodies soon develop diseases from contaminated foods and polluted water."

"However, that is enough for today," Sir Cellular said, sighing with a sense of satisfaction. "Look who is coming to visit our school."

The Starians looked around and saw Mother Htrae moving toward them, arrayed in all the good things of their planet.

Oh, my stars in heaven," she exclaimed when she saw the Htrae family. "You are growing up quickly. Just the same, I am not going to allow Sir Cellular to have you all the time. Come, I want to take you to a special event that is about to occur. It appears the vegetables are going to have a parade, so we must hurry. We certainly must never be discourteous to those who are waiting for us, whether it is in the classroom or on the parade grounds."

CHAPTER VII

Parade of the Vegetables

A blue sky dotted with patches of white clouds greeted the Starians as they came out of the classroom and made their way to the parade ground. They felt the warmth of the sun that had once been their home. Occasionally, when they felt its rays gently enfold them they remembered their happy days there. Then they would look up at the sky and wave to let those not yet brought into being and those just starting life, know they were not forgotten. When the Starians did this they felt at one with everything, and this reminded them that the Lord of the Stars had not forgotten them either.

Mother Htrae led the Starians to the edge of an area where there were no trees and asked them to be seated. Sebastian, Cedric, Jason and all of the others were filled with great curiosity and wondered what new adventure awaited them. As they sat closely together on a thick carpet of green grass, Sir Cellular slipped up quietly and joined them.

In the meantime the vegetables had lined up at the end of the clearing in preparation for their demonstration. They were a most unusual sight, for they had suddenly become enormous and were now even larger than the Starians. This special magic somewhat reminded the Htrae family of their dinosaur days.

"How did they get so big, Mother Htrae?" Franklin asked.

Mother Htrae's eyes twinkled merrily. "Why, Franklin, what a question to ask! They grow big by thinking big, just as you did when you built the great hulks long ago."

"But vegetables are not that big, at least not the ones we eat," commented Joan.

"That is quite true," Sir Cellular responded. "They have obviously expanded to their current size just for this special occasion by using a bit magic from the Lord of the Stars."

"Now, of course," Mother Htrae interjected, "you realize that what you think plays an important role in your life. For instance, if you always thought that you were fat, you could become fat; and if you believe that you can do some special thing, then you can. On the other hand, if you think you can't, then, of course, it would be impossible."

"The vegetables must have grown to that size by an expansion of molecules," Sebastian said thoughtfully. "This would mean that they are not really solid either, but only appear to be."

Mother Htrae looked at Sebastian tenderly and said, "Someday, Sebastian, you will be a great man on Htrae. You do not know this, but once upon a time our little Earth friends had someone much like you. Just like you, he asked a lot of questions and taught new things. Sadly this made people bodies angry with him and one day the angry ones felt they had to kill him. In fact, people planets often have a habit of doing this to their great people.

"Why is that?" asked Cedric.

"It happens that human nature is somewhat governed by its remaining animal tendencies," Mother Htrae responded sadly. "Yet as a flower grows from a seed, so too will humans one day rise above such things. Then, they will cease being human. Greatness lives in everyone and in every thing, but it takes work and patience to develop it."

"Obviously we must work very hard to insure that Htrae will always love its great people and learn from them," Sally stated.

When they heard these words everyone fell silent so they could ponder on the expanded state of the vegetables. Sitting at the edge of the parade grounds, the Starians created a most unusual sight. First, there was Sir Cellular with all his cells moving constantly within him; next sat Sebastian and the others with their destinies protruding from their heads, and last of all was Mother Htrae with her great hat of fresh fruit. Of course, at the end of the parade grounds were the vegetables, which were now enormous as they prepared for review. Yet, in spite of the strange spectacle the group made there was also a sense of excitement floating through the air.

When the vegetables saw their guests patiently waiting for them they quickly went into formation under the direction of Colonel Carrot. Thump! Thump! Thump! The ground shook as they began their march, "Left foot, right foot, left foot, right foot, forward ho!" the Colonel called out with a booming voice.

First in line were the carrots, parsley, onions, cabbage, and parsnips. Further back in the line were the tomatoes, squash, potatoes, and green beans. Behind these came the fruit, displaying colors of orange, gold, pink and red. It was quite an amazing sight to see the huge vegetables and fruits moving in perfect step.

When Cedric said that they looked like one great big stew, Sebastian began philosophizing on how the vegetables grow up to give their lives to people and help them to build bodies without complaining. Of course, Jason heard music in the great thump-thumps, while Franklin wondered if he could expand himself enough to float through the sky.

Paying little attention to the males, the feminine aspects of the Htrae family looked at things somewhat differently. Joan and Sally admired the beauty of all the colors mixed together and wondered how the Lord of the Stars had managed to make each one so different, yet so beautiful. This gave Sally an idea for creating dyes from the vegetables and fruits, which would enable everyone to wear clothes of different colors. So far they had all pretty much dressed in green, like the grass and leaves.

As they all sat in a row, Mother Htrae's glance landed on Franklin. This caused her to shake her head again, and she wondered how many trees he would fall out of before he found a way to fly. Perhaps, she thought, he might even get accidentally electrocuted when he created electric lights.

Although this momentarily appeared to be a rather shocking thought, she was aware of life's continuity and knew that errors in judgment were often man's best teacher.

Turning back to the fruit and vegetables now marching toward them on the parade route, Mother Htrae smiled, because everything was really quite perfect.

As the vegetables neared the onlookers, Colonel Carrot called out; "Halt!" and the members of the parade members came to an abrupt stop. When he called out, "Left and about face," all of the vegetables turned toward those watching the review and bowed.

When the vegetables stopped marching, Colonel Carrot approached the viewers and spoke. "Greetings everyone, we have put this parade on to entertain you, as well as to teach the importance of our role on Htrae. As you know, we appear as food because that is the role assigned to us we by the Lord of the Stars. We actually find it a joy to help you grow so that *Operation Earth Angel* can be completed."

"I don't think I will ever be able to eat another vegetable," Sally declared. "Until today, I just thought of you as something provided for us by Mother Htrae."

"Sally, please don't change your feelings about us just because we are unable to talk in our normal size. The real us are actually never what you eat anyway. You eat only our outer forms. It does please us, however, to have this special day to help you understand our function in maintaining healthy bodies. As you see, it is really only a bit of magic."

"We are very glad we can talk to you, too, Colonel Carrot, particularly since you have long been my favorite vegetable." Sebastian commented.

Colonel Carrot's eyes twinkled, "Frankly, Sebastian, I am quite aware of your extreme fondness for carrots, but you know you had better be careful or you might end up looking just like us. Remember what happens to you when you think. It is important that you learn to love all vegetables, because each one has a special place in your life. Within each vegetable is a special quality which fills some physiological need." "Joan," Colonel Carrot nodded his head toward her. "What is the vegetable you dislike most?"

"Colonel Carrot, I really like them all. However, I know that people bodies on some of the planets dislike spinach a great deal," she replied.

Colonel Carrot stood up very straight and ordered Mrs. Spinach to march to the front ranks and come to attention. "Mrs. Spinach," the Colonel requested, "there are some people in the universe who are not very fond of you. Perhaps if they really got to know you better it would be different, so why don't you tell us something about yourself?"

Mrs. Spinach indicated that it rather saddened her when people bodies did not really like her very much. She knew that lack of understanding had something to do with this. On some planets, people fell into curious eating habits and this caused them to lose their taste for many vegetables. There seemed to be only one-way to overcome such a problem, and that was to teach a better way of life to everyone. With that thought in mind, Mrs. Spinach stood up very straight and began to tell about herself.

"You will notice that my clothes are comprised of green leaves," she began. "My leaves are not this color by accident, but they are green because they are made of sunlight which I absorb and store. I am also different from Colonel Carrot, as he grows beneath the surface of the land and I grow above the ground. This means that our nutritional values are different. In other words, I provide different vitamins and minerals than carrots. For instance, I have more calcium than eggs and milk, but less phosphorous than Brussels sprouts."

For a moment Mrs. Spinach paused to catch her breath, but seeing how attentive everyone was she quickly continued. "Usually people think of me as being very high in iron; however, I really have only half as much as an avocado. As a good source of calcium, however, I aid in the formation of bones and teeth and serve as a first aid station to stop excessive bleeding. With my good content of phosphorous, I assist in nervous conditions, and with iron I aid in oxygen transmission.

"Quite frankly, many people do not know that spinach is ranked second in the mineral called sodium which aids in digestion, and helps overcome a very dreaded disease called arthritis. There is only one other vegetable higher in sodium and that is celery."

"Then a person who eats an abundance of spinach would actually have better teeth, be less nervous, and be more energetic!" cried Sally.

"Yes, and more, Sally," Mrs. Spinach continued. "I rank second highest in magnesium which builds lung tissue and helps in cleansing waste products from the body. As one of the highest sources of sulfur, one of my more important functions is forming proteins and normalizing heart action. My chlorine aids in decreasing weight, while my silicon is found in human tissue." She shook her head. "We haven't even discussed vitamins yet."

"Mrs. Spinach, we really would like to know all about your vitamins too," Sally begged, "that is, if you do not mind."

"All right, Sally, if you really want to know. Yet, you must remember that I am no more special than other vegetables and fruits. When you know their story, you will find that they are equally important. For instance, our friend Mr. Tomato over there is the best-known source of potassium, many times more than the banana. He is also the highest source of magnesium, aiding in convulsions, digestion, and complexion disorders. So you see we are really somewhat like people. If everyone would learn to stress only the good, you would find that each person is special, too."

"What a wonderful lesson, Mrs. Spinach. It seems that every-thing living has special lessons to teach if we would only learn to listen," Sally commented.

"That is quite true, Sally," Sir Cellular interjected. "It is called the study of Natural Law."

"Then Natural Law will become my favorite study," Sally added.

Mother Htrae looked gently at Sally and spoke. "Be careful about that, Sally, because there is always a chance you may give too much attention to one study and this would limit you. Learn each subject well, but never forget there are other lessons to be learned and other teachers to learn from. After all, nature is actu-ally no more than a suit of clothes which Lord of the Stars wears."

With this Mrs. Spinach smiled and prepared to continue her story. "Let's see now," she went on slowly as though she were think-ing. "Spinach ranks second in Vitamin A, so it helps to prolong life and aids resistance toward infections. Of course, my vitamin B-1 soothes nerves and spurs growth, while my high content of vitamin B-2 is indispensable to cell restoration. And this may re-ally surprise you, but I contain much more vitamin C than an orange or any other fruit, even though fruit is also very important in the diet. Vitamin C in spinach helps protect the vascular system and plays a defensive role against bacterial toxins."

"You would say, that people who have a bad heart, weak lungs, poor appetites, anemia, bad teeth, swollen joints, gastric ulcers, intestinal infections, and who are tired and nervous should all really learn to depend on your help," Sebastian reflected. "In all of these diseases, you help people bodies to get well, and also aid in keeping them from getting ill in the first place."

"Of course we all know that poor food may often seem to taste better than good things like Mrs. Spinach. What can we do about that?" asked Franklin.

"Why Franklin," chided Mother Htrae, "don't forget you become what you think. If everyone would just remember the good qualities of vegetables and fruits, soon no one would want to eat poorly."

"But, Mother Htrae, we have studied the life on other people planets closely and it seems that many people will eat anything that tastes good, particularly something that is not natural.

"Perhaps if we cannot convince them," Colonel Carrot spoke up, "other members of the fruit and vegetable kingdom can. Therefore, let us continue with the parade." Looking up for a moment now, Colonel Carrot peered at the Starians with great affection and said, "Although we may never be able to talk again in this manner, I want you to know that we are always happy to take care of you." With this he called out the order to continue the parade. "Company; come to attention. Right face – forward, march."

The thump-thump-thump of the marching vegetables and fruits could be heard very far away as they passed by the viewers one after another introducing themselves.

"I am Mrs. Onion and I help calm nerves," the first lady said.

Left foot, right foot. I am Miss Asparagus, and I help increase your life span," said the next one, rather slender, but proud.

"Hello, I am Mrs. Kale, rich in chlorine and sulfur which helps in maintaining normal heart action." another called as she passed in review.

One after another they marched — cabbage, turnips, and beet greens. Then a rather strange bunch of green leaves stopped and said, "I am Mrs. Dandelion, and I am actually a vegetable although many people kill me because they think of me as a weed. I am very high in vitamin A, which helps in growth and maintaining healthy glands, and I am richer in vitamin C than fruit. My high calcium content helps to build strong teeth, but I also contain a good source of iron, which is capable of fighting anemia. Even my copper is necessary for respiration."

At this point, Mrs. Dandelion had to pause to breath because she had a great deal to say. When she had taken a deep breath, she continued, saying, "These leaves you see are much higher in potassium than a banana, and actually aid in prevention of goiters, as well as assist in the biological function of the thyroid. My magnesium helps to build strong bones."

Yet," Mrs. Dandelion paused again and shook her head sorrowfully, "although it is possible for me to help many people, I am afraid I am usually looked upon as quite a pest."

"Don't ever worry about not being liked on Htrae," Sally spoke up. "Whenever we pick your yellow flowers, we will also pick your leaves and eat them."

"Be careful Sally," Mrs. Dandelion cautioned. "If you don't pick me when my leaves are young and tender, I can be quite difficult to chew. Also, I have a tendency to multiply very rapidly, so I need to be harvested before my seeds get blown away by the wind." After she returned to her position in line, Colonel Carrot gave the command to move forward again.

As the vegetables continued their march and neared the end of the parade ground, they began to diminish. Soon they had returned to their normal size, their magic finished.

Cedric immediately jumped up and headed for the forest classroom.

"Where are you going, Cedric?" asked Mother Htrae.

"Why, Mother Htrae, you know! You told me to listen to everything, and one day my music would become very great. I am off to write a splendid symphony, called 'The Parade of the Vegetables'!" answered Cedric.

The other Starians followed more slowly. Sebastian, who was always thinking, asked, "Did you notice something strange about the vegetables that stopped to talk to us?"

"Oh, no, I thought they were all so very wonderful, though the parade would never have been as beautiful without the lovely fruit." answered Sally. "Why do you ask?"

"I noticed something quite unusual," Sebastian replied. "While all varieties of fruit and vegetables passed in review, most of those who spoke to us were vegetables that are not well liked on people planets."

"Quite true, Sebastian," Mother Htrae quietly agreed. "It simply shows us that everything has a divine purpose and should be accepted. If people bodies only continued to eat what they like most of the time, then it would not be a proper diet. Soon many good things could no longer live. If each planetary child and each Starian learned to enjoy those vegetables and fruit they have not liked, then it would not be long before they would learn to like everything. Why, some plants which are considered weeds are actually herbs and heal people's bodies of illnesses, almost like magic."

"Would you give us an example of that, Mother Htrae," requested Franklin.

"That is a lesson for another time, Franklin. Herbs must be used as medicines in a sensible and knowledgeable manner. But come now, nature is beginning to sleep and so must all of you."

As the Starians lay down on their beds and closed their eyes, the memories of their friends on parade stayed with them. They knew that they would try very hard to live that which they had been taught.

High in the heavens, the Lord of the Stars kept vigil over all the planets and smiled tenderly at the Starians through the gentle moonlight.

CHAPTER VIII

Professor Biogenics

The sixth epoch of progression was passing rapidly and each morning brought countless new adventures for the Htrae family. Joan and Sally had created sewing and the clothes everyone wore now were dyed the colors of various vegetables and fruits. Franklin, who had never given up his dream of flying, had invented a new type of glue. He was certain that his new invention would hold his rather futuristic feathered wings together. Nonetheless, Franklin had not overlooked the needs of those who lived on Htrae. He had invented more practical things such as a round wheel, plows, and wagons, and these inventions revolutionized Htrae.

While Franklin dreamed up his new inventions, the music of Cedric and the art of Jason also improved. Both music and art had become a major form of entertainment for everyone who dwelled on the planet.

About this time, the astronomers on Earth discovered Htrae through their telescopes. Immediately there was a great deal of speculation about this new planet appearing in the heavens. Some thought Htrae was about the same size as Earth, although they were quite puzzled by its unusual behavioral pattern. Most planets made systematic journeys around the sun and held strictly to their routine orbital paths. Htrae, on the other hand, not only seemed to be rotating within the sun's massive vortex in an elliptical pattern, but also appeared to be coming nearer to Earth each day.

When the information concerning the planet was released to the press, some of the Earth humans believed that it was a sign of the end of the world. Others felt that a miracle was about to happen.

While the excitement of Htrae's discovery was occurring on earth, outside a distant forest classroom the Mother of Htrae and Sir Cellular were preparing the Starians for a new course of study known as Biogenics, or the study of living food. It had been some time since either one of them had shared the education of a new planet with their old friend, Professor Biogenics. Both teachers felt that the Starians would enjoy learning about living food from the creator of Biogenic Science. Therefore, they agreed that Professor Biogenics should be summoned to the classroom immediately.

This task was accomplished by projecting a thought invitation through the ether and into Professor's consciousness, although he was a few light years away. Because thought travels faster than the speed of light, one is instantly where one thinks. Thus, very little time passed before Professor Biogenics, having received the message, joined Sir Cellular and Mother Htrae in a green pavilion just a short distance from the classroom. In fact, almost as soon as the two of them opened their eyes they saw their long time friend and associate materialize right in front of them.

"How wonderful to see you both," the Professor said, as he began to solidify his body. "Earlier I was notified by Ambassador Marius that I would probably be called upon to help the Starians in their education. I do not know when I have had a mission that seemed so important. *Operation Earth Angel* is perhaps one of the most unique plans to happen in this particular solar system, perhaps even the Galaxy. It would be difficult not to want to be a part of it."

Professor Biogenics presented a rather imposing sight as he stood in front of Sir Cellular and Mother Htrae. His body was a yellow square and his hair was comprised of bright green wheat grass. Beneath his body appeared two rather spindly, but wiry legs. The Professor always explained that these allowed him complete flexibility, because any inability to be flexible often caused great harm to those who were rigid and set in their ways. Also, he wore large square glasses, which were balanced on the end his nose in a most remarkable fashion. In size and shape they were very similar to those that Sebastian wore. Certainly the glasses gave Professor Biogenics a very distinguished look. In spite of them, however, his dark eyes could pierce even the deepest secrets of the soul

"My old friend, it is good to see you," Sir Cellular replied. "Indeed we have sent for you. This planet has reached human evolution and must learn to build refined people bodies. The bodies that the Starians now possess vibrate much too densely to become divine and this must change if they are to save earth. Although we realize that you are very busy, and in great demand, it would be quite a loss to the Starians not to have the benefit of your wisdom."

The Professor paused for a few minutes, as if in deep thought. Then he looked at Sir Cellular and Mother Htrae, and nodded his head. "Naturally I am delighted to be here and would not miss this opportunity. I will be happy to stay as long as I am needed, but then I must return to earth. You probably already know that I have been working with some of the Earthlings for quite some time. This is to ascertain that certain groundwork is accomplished in time for the Starians fulfill their mission."

Later, as they walked side by side to the forest classroom, Mother Htrae asked, "Professor, how is Earth these days? Do you think she will be ready in time?"

Of course, it was well known throughout the galaxies that Professor was an inveterate optimist. He maintained this status by nodding his head again, saying, "I think so. You would actually be quite amazed at some of the things taking place throughout much of Earth."

"My, I am delighted to hear that," Mother Htrae responded softly.

By this time the three of them had reached the forest classroom where the Starians had assembled. They took their seats in front of the group and then Sir Cellular stood up to introduce the Professor.

"Students, this is Professor Biogenics who has been kind enough to come here and teach a course on the science of living foods. Professor not only knows a great deal about cell life, but he also has an unusual ability to speak the various languages of the plant and animal world. I am quite certain you will enjoy your studies with him."

Sir Cellular's introduction to Professor Biogenics was met with blinking eyes and gapping mouths, for the Starians' new teacher was even more unusual in appearance than the others had been. Although they found Professor's bright yellow square body sufficiently astounding, it was his green wheat grass hair that brought absolute disbelief and silence to the classroom.

The Professor was well aware of the student's amazement as he rose to greet them, and his eyes lit up with humor. He became even more amused as he watched the Starians bob their heads to and fro in an effort to keep their eyes focused on him. Since his legs were extremely spindly, he swayed back and forth much as a field of grass blowing in the summer wind. For this reason, the Starians had to pay strict attention in an effort to keep track of him.

"You see," Professor Biogenics began, "when people become fixed in their opinion, or become narrow minded, they close the doors to progress. This in turn brings separation between themselves and others. However, if everyone would grow like the grass, the flowers, and the trees, they would be flexible and bend in the wind of new ideas. As a scientist, I make it a practice to keep up with planetary progress. Therefore, my legs have become an expressions of my ability to study all new ideas."

Sir Cellular nodded his head in agreement, as did some of the Starians when they recovered their wits. "That is certainly correct, Professor," said Sir Cellular, "I have watched what happens to those who unfortunately become inflexible because of their habits and opinions. Nevertheless, this problem has occurred throughout every aspect of civilization, even in science, religion, medicine, school systems, and politics. I realize that those who get caught in such a web are not aware that they actually hold up the progress of everything throughout the universe of the stars. I'm afraid that I find it quite unfortunate at times."

Professor Biogenics looked at Sir Cellular with deep understanding, for they had both seen many great people persecuted and even killed over new ideas. "But, we must also remember this" the Professor responded, "New ideas are a sign of growth and exploration in the evolutionary process of any planet. Those who do not understand this hurt themselves more than those they persecute. After all, the Lord of the Stars lives within all life and it must ultimately progress and learn all unlearned lessons. The forward movement of the Great Plan cannot be stopped."

Pausing for a few moments, the Professor looked over the classroom to make certain that everyone understood what he was saying. Then he continued, "As you know, some ideas really do not work very well, but when this happens new concepts have to be explored. There is actually no real failure. Perhaps Franklin will not find a way to fly, but his work will help someone else to do so in the future. Instead of laughing at those who are different, every person would find a great deal of happiness by embracing the world of discovery."

As Professor talked, Starians watched the gold and green apparition moving back and forth in the breeze. Although they were thinking very deeply about what he was saying, they were also beginning to realize that even the oddest-looking creatures seemed to have their own special lessons to impart to those who are willing to listen.

The scientist continued to sway as he spoke, and sometimes when he got excited, he looked as though he was about to take off and fly. "It is my responsibility to teach you about living foods and the unborn seed children," he continued. "Although you already know the value of vegetables and fruits, you may not know that a very long time ago a Persian sage on Earth said that the secrets of the universe could be found within a single grain of wheat. He was right, of course."

Sebastian reflected on what he had just heard, for he faintly remembered having heard something about the sage and his grain of wheat. At that time Sebastian had reached the conclusion that seeds actually give birth to new life in much the same manner a sun gives birth to planets.

Suddenly, realizing that his mind had begun to wander, Sebastian immediately turned his attention back to what the Professor was saying.

"As I mentioned," Professor Biogenics continued, "When seed children are planted in the soil, they automatically draw minerals and moisture by the process of harmonics. A seed functions somewhat like a magnet. If one were to pass a magnet over metal filings, they would see that the magnet draws the particles to it. Because seed children emanate the most powerful energy at the time they are being born, or sprouted, we can say they are at their highest point of magnetism. During this time they draw nutrients from the soil in much the same manner as the magnet draws metal filings.

"After the seed's sprouting stage," Professor continued, "each one breaks through the earth's surface and begins to draw in sunlight and air. This starts, what is referred to as a bioactive stage. This is the growth period in which the seed, or to simplify matters -let us say a grain of wheat, begins to prepare for reproduction. Later it will give birth to twenty or thirty grains of wheat much in the manner Lord of the Stars created the universe."

Professor Biogenics paused for a brief moment before concluding his class, and then said, "I believe that is enough for today; we will go on with more tomorrow."

Everyone was talking about magnetism and green hair as they left the classroom. For once it was Franklin who hastened on his way to begin meditation.

"Franklin," Cedric called. "Where are you going so fast?"

Stopping for a few moments, Franklin allowed Cedric, Sebastian, Webster and Jason to catch up. Then he made a very startling announcement. "I am going to practice levitation."

"What are you talking about now, Franklin? I thought you were interested in flying." Jason responded.

"Well, it dawned on me when Professor Biogenics introduced the unborn seed children, that seeds can actually levitate," he answered.

"This is one time you are ahead of me, Franklin," Sebastian laughed, "How about telling us about your ideas."

"Some mysterious power within the wheat makes it possible for it to break through the earth," Franklin replied. "It does so because it does not know it cannot. Therefore, a human body should be able to lift many times its own weight, if it ceases to be aware of the outer form. Of course, if this occurred in a human body, it could also develop weightlessness and levitation would be possible. I am afraid it might take some practice."

Sebastian spoke enthusiastically; "I am going to practice levitation with you, Franklin. Perhaps between the two of us we can figure it out."

"Does this mean you are going to give up flying, Franklin?" Sally asked.

"Not really, Sally," Franklin answered softly. "Actually, in both cases we have to overcome gravity, so levitation would actually be a form of flying. If we learn to levitate, maybe we won't have to invent flying at all."

Everyone from Cedric to Joan decided that levitation was worth a try. Off they went to a clearing not far away to practice forgetting they had a body.

In his station located in the great cosmic sea, Ambassador Marius could barely contain his amusement.

"What is so amusing Ambassador Marius?" asked the Lord of the Stars, who immediately became aware of his Chief Counsel's merriment"

"It is the Starians. They are trying to learn how to levitate," Ambassador Marius replied, "Although they have never forgotten to live our ways, it does seem they have forgotten how to overcome gravity. Do you think we should help them?"

"No," answered the Lord of the Stars. "Not yet. Franklin is a fine inventor and has many wonderful experiences ahead of him. It we help him too much he will not enjoy his success. As you well know, Franklin's role on Htrae will be over as soon as he finds a way to harness solar energy, and while he will not be the first to fly, his ideas will help others succeed."

"That is true," the Ambassador agreed. "At the rate the Starians are growing it will not be long before they will become divine and fulfill their mission."

The next day when Professor stood up in front of the class and cleared his throat, he announced, "Learning to levitate really does not help us to learn love, and it is really very important for all planets to become harmonious. Just imagine a planet of people bodies all floating around while they try to kill each other. Let us first learn the basic fundamentals of the power within us, and how to utilize this power for the good of all life. When the body and mind are subdued, then you can enjoy the power of levitation. That way it will not be only the body which transcends gravity, but also the mind."

The Starians looked at each other in surprise. There was apparently one difficulty with unity; everyone seemed to know what everyone else was doing.

Professor cleared his throat again to draw the attention of the Starians back to their studies. "As we discussed yesterday, when the unborn seed children are planted or soaked in water, they begin to grow, or sprout. At this time they exude more energy than at any other time and are therefore referred too as biogenic.

"The second state of growth for seed children is referred to as bioactive, or food that is still growing but its potency has not been reduced by heat, or cooking. Therefore, it still has an energy source to nourish the human body. You must remember, however, that the longer a food is separated from its life source the less bioactive it is.

The Third phase of growth is considered bio-static, meaning mature protein foods such as rice, lentils and beans. These create necessary biological support for people bodies, but must be cooked. Therefore, at the time they are consumed they are not a living food, yet they do not cause harm to the body.

With these words the Professor got very, very serious. "The final aspect of food is biocidic, or food that causes the human body to become ill. By this I mean some people can actually destroy their own health with improper foods that are void of good nutrients."

While the Starians never indulged in biocidic food, they decided to eat more sprouts because of the Professor's teaching. When they tried this experiment they found that their IQ increased. Sebastian also discovered something else. He found the secret to changing, or transmuting, the body into a higher frequency.

The way Sebastian explained it to the other Starians, "It seems that our true essence is light, but this light is dimmed by a layer of matter. Of course, I am talking about our people bodies. If we eat foods that are of coarse vibration, or which have no life force, the body becomes even denser. This causes a greater separation between the vibration of our true nature and that of our earth body. If we eat high vibratory foods, however, the body becomes refined and more in harmony with its true light body which never ages or dies."

When Sebastian finished speaking, the others looked at him with awe. Then Sally spoke up and said, "Oh! Sebastian, you are so wise, and I do see what you mean. By transmuting, or refining our human bodies we can become more one with everything. If I eat sprouts, those sprouts in me would unite with the grasses and trees and draw their energy into me. This would not only help sustain my life, but would also help eliminate illnesses because our true nature is never ill."

"Yes Sally, all that is true," Sebastian replied, "Or at least I believe the concept is reasonable."

Not long thereafter Sebastian's idea proved valid. One day when the Starians were studying with Professor Biogenics, he did discuss body transmutation and said, "A body filled with impure food hurts more when it is injured than that of a body fed on biogenic and bioactive food. To better understand this, you might consider your organo-vegetative bodies to be somewhat like a group of musical keys on a piano with high notes and low notes.

"Although the body is a wonderful creation, those that vibrate at a more dense level develop diseases more readily and is more painful when injured. This means that pain moves through a lower vibratory frequency more slowly than pain moving through a higher vibratory frequency. The same goes for the aging process, for the higher the vibration of the body is the slower it breaks down. And. it also heals much more readily," Professor added.

Webster raised his hand. "Professor, does this mean that a people body can reach a point where it never dies?"

"Webster," the Professor answered, "it is really not that simple, at least at Htrae's current stage of evolution. You must understand that the body is a suit of clothes, and it will always be somewhat heavier than your true Starian forms. Some day, however, you will lay your people bodies aside forever because your work on Htrae will be finished."

At this point Professor Biogenics stopped, cleared his throat and looked very mysterious. "In worlds beyond this one you will want the form of that world and will not desire people bodies."

Then the Professor closed his book and winked at Mother Htrae. The two of them departed from the platform together. It was the first time that other worlds in the galaxy had been mentioned in the Starians' earth classroom in such a way, although they had learned quite a bit concerning them from Ambassador Marius.

As the Htrae family left the classroom, day had begun to turn into night and the gleaming light of Lord of the Stars shown through millions of light windows.

"Just imagine," Webster mused, "all the time Earth's adventurer, Ponce de Leon, searched for the fountain of youth it lived within him."

The other Starians did not hear this because they had begun to ponder the mystery of other worlds. Out of the billions of galaxy families residing in the Lord of the Stars, they decided there must be planets much more evolved than either Earth or Htrae.

CHAPTER IX

Brother Arbo

The Starians continued with daily lessons in order to prepare for *Operation Earth Angel*, and during this time life
remained good. Nonetheless, the twists and turns of planetary building would soon bring them to another teacher, Hermano
Arbo. Hermano Arbo, meaning *Brother Tree*, dwelled deep in the
Great North Woods. He had retired there two thousand years
earlier after teaching the ancient ones who once lived on earth. To
Mother Htrae and Old Gusty, the wind, he was remembered as
the Tree of Life and considered one of the greatest ecological wisdoms in the galaxies. They revered him highly and had abided by
his wishes that he be left quietly to his contemplations.

Now, however, Brother Arbo's contemplative life was about to
change, for the Lord of the Stars had a new assignment for him,
one that would teach him to be more loving. Certainly it was well
known that the great tree had lost some of its humanitarian aspects and could be quite difficult to get along with.

The disturbance to Hermano Arbo's contemplative life occurred one day during the Starians' search for trees to use in building homes. They had been led deep into the North Woods by their faithful friend, Gusty, the wind, whom they loved and trusted. The Starians were exceptionally fond of the Gusty, for he not only served as a cooling system for the Lord of the Stars, but he also brought back exciting stories back about life on Earth. By day he played hide and seek with the sun, and by night Gusty sang some of the ballads he had written about life in the galaxies. Even though Sebastian and all the others realized that the Old Gusty had a tendency to exaggerate on occasion, they easily forgave him for this.

On this day Old Gusty had little-by-little led the Htrae family deeper into the forest. The Starians enjoyed watching him playing among the branches of the trees, and they became enraptured with the dance of the flowers. Thus, they were quite surprised when Gusty told them that they were about to make a new acquaintance.

The group followed him merrily, full of curiosity and anticipating the new adventure. It was a beautiful day and before long everyone began singing the Starian ballad, which Jason had composed. Sally started singing first and was quickly joined by the others.

Singing occupied the attention of group so much that they did not notice they had passed the less dense section of the forest. They were now an area where the trees stood close together and were heavily moss laden. Suddenly, looming before them was the largest tree the Starians had ever seen. They came to an abrupt stop and looked up at it. The tree rose so high toward the sky that everyone had to twist their people necks to see the top, and its trunk was so huge that Sebastian had to walk around it just to see the forest on the other side. Its size was not the only outstanding feature, but it also seemed to have eyes in every leaf and a huge knothole heart.

As the Starians stood gaping, their mouths open, a rumbling began. The ground shook and the leaf eyes took on a glowering look. Sebastian and Jason noticed that all of them seemed to express an exact reflection of the tree's larger eyes, which now stared down on them with an extraordinary amount of irritation. Abruptly the great tree spoke; its voice was deep and gruff. "Well, what are you gaping at?" he demanded.

Quite startled, Joan jumped back. "We are looking at you. Why, you must be the largest tree on the whole planet."

The great tree appeared to think about this for a moment, although Joan could see that the idea of being the largest tree on the whole planet seemed to please it. Then the tree asked, "And just who might you be?"

"Well, Mr. Tree, we are Starians and we are wearing people bodies," Joan tried to explain. "You see, we live on Htrae and have been sent into the universe on a special mission to help Earth."

"Harrumph!" growled the tree, shaking his leaves. "From what Gusty tells me, Earth needs all the help it can get. In fact, the people there have been destroying so many of us that their ecology is suffering an imbalance."

"What do you mean Earth's treeology is suffering?" asked Webster, who was as usual very interested in new words.

The great tree mumbled irritably. "That's ecology, not treeology. It is really a long story and very complicated, so I would rather not go into the matter. Besides, you would probably not understand.

"By the way, I would prefer that you not call me 'Mr. Tree' for I am actually your brother. I may not have the same form you have, but the Lord of the Stars created me just as he created you. I too have been on special assignment, which began long before you even had body forms. Therefore, in the future, if there is a future, kindly call me *Hermano Arbo*, or *Brother Arbo* if it easier for you.

"Actually," Brother Arbo added, looking quite pleased, "Gusty the Wind tells me, that when Professor Biogenics once lived on earth in human form he wrote a book about me called, *Hermano Arbo*, which in the Spanish language means *Brother Tree*. I understand that he did quite a good job of writing it, in spite of the fact that he did not ask my advice."

With this thought, the tree took on an even a grumpier appearance.

"I imagine you have many stories to tell," Franklin remarked. "I know that we would all like to hear them. Perhaps you will consider telling them to us sometime."

"Harrumph. Harrumph," Brother Arbo answered rather rudely. "I will have to think about that. In the meantime, I would be quite interested in learning how you found me. I have lived in these woods for thousands of years in peace and quiet. Now you come strolling along, singing at the top of your lungs, scaring all the animals in my keeping and upsetting my contemplation."

Sebastian took over as spokesman for the group. "Please let me explain, Brother Arbo. Our cave homes are no longer suitable for our changing forms. We have found that homes built of wood are more comfortable, so we often come here to cut down trees for building houses."

At this Brother Arbo let out a great series of harrumphs and grumps, and became so agitated that the ground began shaking again. When he had finally quieted down somewhat, he said irritably, "You mean you destroy us just to build a house to live in? Well, they have done that on many people planets and it has always created trouble. Without trees a planet becomes stark and desolate. Eventually, everything becomes no more than a desert and then all living things began to die. In spite of this you come into my Forest and want to do the same thing."

With these words the great tree shook its branches wildly and mumbled, "I won't have it. I simply won't have it."

Realizing that he had somewhat frightened the Starians, Brother Arbo eventually quieted down again and said. "I must assume that Gusty has something to do with this invasion on my privacy. He is inclined to whip things up a bit every place he goes, and seldom allows me little peace and quiet when he is around."

"Wait, Brother Arbo," Sebastian cried out. "We really mean no harm. Professor Biogenics and Mother Htrae have taught us to be very careful in selecting wood so that we do not damage the forest. Besides, we always plant special tree seeds in order to replace what we take."

Such facts did little to appease the gruffness of Brother Arbo. Other planets had taught similar things to their families. Yet when a planet had progressed to human development its human life forms seemed determined to upset the ecology anyway by building great concrete structures. Therefore, the tree decided that it would be best to remain silent and try to ignore the entire interruption, assuming it was nearly over.

After making this decision, a deep silence settled over the North Woods and Brother Arbo no longer communicated with his visitors. The Starians, thinking they had upset the tree so much that he would no longer talk to them, turned and walked away in disappointment.

As Sebastian and the others turned away, Ambassador Marius suddenly appeared before the old tree and chastised it. "Hermano Arbo, how could you do this to your guests? After all, this planet is a special planet and I have allowed you to rein supreme over the other trees because you are older and wiser. You have much to teach these young humans and I would be saddened if you did not do what you could to help them with *Operation Earth Angel*."

For a moment the Ambassador paused, and then a mischievous hint of a smile touched his lips, "Perhaps you would rather become a novelty shop like your counterpart in Earth's Redwood Forest?"

When Brother Arbo heard these words he was horrified. How could the Lord of the Stars do this to him, after all he had done? Nevertheless, he knew that the Ambassador was not pleased with him. It seemed that no matter how he felt about the matter, he, Hermano Arbo, giant of the forest, would have to forsake the peaceful existence he had become accustomed to.

Just as the Starians reached the path which lead out of the woods, they heard Hermano Arbo grumbling in a distance.

"Come back, come back," the tree called out."

The group turned around and made their way back to Brother Arbo. After they arrived, they took standing positions near his huge trunk. Having already learned how irritable he could be, however, the Starians decided it was better not speak until he spoke.

When the Hermano Arbo saw the Franklin, Cedric, Joan and the others standing in front of him again, he said, "I just had a visit from someone you all know, Ambassador Marius."

At this point, Brother Arbo explained, not wishing to admit openly that he had been criticized, "The Ambassador has suggested that I teach you. Apparently, you are being prepared for something called *Operation Earth Angel* and may need all of the help that you can get. Since I am not familiar with such an operation, perhaps one of you would explain exactly what that means."

Sebastian, the Starians' usual spoke's person, began to explain, "As we understand it, Earth is about to graduate and become divine. However, the humans on Earth apparently do not know who they really are. Therefore, many of them keep fighting and bickering with one another, not to count their strong attraction for earthly things rather than heavenly things. They do not realize that their planet is headed toward the asteroid belt and that they must graduate before reaching it. If we do not help them, Earth will disintegrate and become thousands of asteroids. If this occurs, the pre-conditions for life on their planet will not exist."

"Harrumph," Brother Arbo muttered and shook his leaves again to show that the news disturbed him. He wondered if humans ever really learned.

As he harrumphed the Starians stepped back, expecting the ground to start shaking. When this did not happen they gathered close to the tree trunk again and waited.

Looking down on them with a measure of skepticism because he did not think humans were extremely intelligent, Hermano Arbo said, "Then I suppose I must help you. You certainly will not be able to accomplish *Operation Earth Angel* without me. However, you must understand that I have not taught since I instructed the ancient predecessors of earth thousands of years ago."

As he remembered his ancient friends, Brother Arbo beamed proudly and asked, "You have, of course, heard about the great ones who once lived on Earth, haven't you?"

The Starians shook their heads, which caused Brother Arbo to wonder if the Starians knew anything at all. "No wonder planets get into trouble," he thought. "It seems that when souls become bound to people bodies they have to learn the ways of the Lord of the Stars all over again."

Thereupon the great tree shook his branches again, knowing that he must either teach these Starians, who were now looking up at him, or face the possibility of being turned into a novelty store. Thus he decided that it was in his best interest to continue speaking. "From time-to-time there have been very special souls who have gone to live on Earth. Such beings always work to show others a better way of life, although they are often misunderstood. Actually some of the ancient ones even used me as a symbol to represent the proper use of Natural and Cosmic forces and referred to me as the 'Tree of Life'. From studying my ways they learned some of the hidden mysteries of the universe."

"What do you mean, studying your ways?" asked Sally.

Brother Arbo again wondered if these people bodies standing

before him knew anything. Harrumphing again, although with less agitation, he asked, "And may I ask what your name is?"

"My name is Sally." She responded.

"Well, Sally, to answer to your question. For instance, if people raised their eyes toward the Lord of the Stars and heaven, as I raise my branches toward the sky, a soul would draw the heavenly forces to them such as power, love and wisdom. This would in turn unite them with the consciousness of the Lord of the Stars and they would become very intelligent, somewhat like Ambassador Marius. On the other hand, if people took nutrients from the earth as I take mine from the earth, their bodies would last longer and be healthier."

When he heard the words power, love and wisdom, Sebastian became even more attentive. After many years of study with Mother Htrae, Sebastian knew that one of the major problems with people bodies on many planets was their inability to live in harmony with nature. Although most people bodies worshipped the Lord of the Stars in some form, they were not able to value him in all forms. Thus, Sebastian spoke for all the Starians when he said, "We have studied with many teachers and I believe I can speak for all of us; it would certainly be a great honor for us to study with the Tree of Life."

At the word "honor" the great tree straightened up his branches a bit. "Perhaps," he thought, "there is hope for these Starians after all."

By this time the ideas of teaching again was beginning to appeal to Brother Arbo. He felt that he might be able to clear up some misunderstandings about angels and mysterious trees. From Gusty, the Brother Arbo had learned that many people bodies on many planets did not know the forces such as sun, air and water were looked upon as heavenly forces. The few who had managed to learn to live in harmony with these forces usually helped others, and became fine healers, prophets, and teachers.

"Yes," Brother Arbo thought, "people who have not discovered their origin surely get mixed up."

Once again, restored to his rightful place as ruler of the forest, Hermano Arbo looked at the Starians somewhat more kindly. "Come early each day before your planetary work begins," he told them, "and I will teach you as I once taught the ancient ones before they descended to earth."

After making this statement, the great tree again grew silent and spoke no more. The Starians finally gave up getting any additional information. Turning away they returned to the path leading out of the great North Woods.

The next morning, the sun had barely risen above the hills when the Htrae family gathered outside of Sebastian's door in preparation for their trek into the woods. They did not wish to keep Brother Arbo waiting, particularly since they knew that his disposition could be a bit trying.

Mother Htrae smiled to herself as she watched Sally, Joan and all the others hurry off. She knew that trees had much to teach everyone, and she sensed that the group was going to meet with Brother Arbo. Nonetheless she was somewhat surprised that old tree had decided to teach again. As she pondered on the matter, she was shown Ambassador Marius' visit with Brother Arbo the day before, and the subtle threat he made about turning the tree into a novelty shop. This caused Mother Htrae a great deal of amusement.

"Harrumph!" Brother Arbo grunted as he saw his new students coming towards him. "It is about time you got here." He lifted a furtive knothole eye toward the sky to insure that they were not too late. His former students had always been early risers and he was used to punctuality. Just the same, he felt that it was somewhat pleasant to be teaching again, even if it was helping him to avoid the fate of his Earth Brother in the Redwoods.

Motioning the students to sit down, Hermano Arbo began. "You notice that my trunk has many branches pointed toward the sky. This symbolizes my eternal growth towards the light. The roots of my current form also absorb from the soil to meet my needs, just as you eat things from the land to sustain your people bodies. Since I have life, and I, as well as other trees produce living things such as leaves and fruit, we are really no more trees than you are people bodies. We are in truth spirit and a part of Lord of the Stars."

As usual, Sebastian was very interested in the possibility that Brother Arbo was not really a tree. "You mean then that your exterior form and people bodies are actually very similar; both absorbing whatever is necessary from the surface of the planet to build an outer form."

Brother Arbo added another "harrumph" at Sebastian's comment, but inside his knothole heart he felt he might have actually found an apt student. Sebastian did remind the teacher somewhat of the ancients he had once taught on Earth.

The teacher replied, "That is correct, Sebastian, but there is much more to me than that. Spirit or energy flows through matter and produces a force field, which is sometimes referred to as an aura or energy pattern. Of course, everything has one including people, flowers, and trees. The more inanimate the life form, meaning something which has been disconnected from its major life source, the smaller the energy field surrounding it. People bodies have the most colorful auras because their thoughts, health, and personalities all affect them.

"Now take the trees for instance," said Brother Arbo, waving his branches with pride, "we have a large energy field which actually helps supply oxygen to an entire planet; therefore, people who are surrounded by trees feel better and live longer."

"Oh, I see," announced Joan. "If there were no trees on Htrae, it would be more difficult for life to exist."

Franklin interjected, "Of course, you are a perfect anti-pollution device because you radiate energy and absorb carbon dioxide, as well as other impurities in the air, and transform them into oxygen."

After hearing Franklin, Sebastian decided to add some of his conclusions on the matter. "Brother Arbo, I imagine that this is all part of the mystery surrounding what you referred to, as good ecology."

Upon hearing this Brother Arbo looked at the Starians seated under his branches with a measure of pride. He had not expected to find them quite so intelligent. "You are all quite correct. Proper ecology means maintaining enough natural forces such as energy from trees, pollination from bees, and oxygen from flowing rivers to maintain healthy life on planets. Where there are more people and factories than the trees, grasses, flowers, and rivers can purify, life is destroyed and must begin again. Actually, if people bodies were careful, they could complete the people cycle of evolution without pollution."

Pausing to look up at the sky, Brother Arbo said, "I see that the sun is rising higher and it is time for you to resume your daily activities. I will see you tomorrow."

As usual, the great tree terminated his conversation with a rumble and a big "Harrumph!"

Because of their experiences the day before, the Starians knew they would get no more out of their new tree teacher at this time. However, they decided to be more careful in the future and insure that there were sufficient trees, grasses, and flowers around the structures they built. It was Sebastian, of course, who worked out a plan for environmental living in the city.

"If the industries were kept in the outlying lands," Sebastian reasoned, "then many trees could be planted and small parks built to serve as anti-pollution stations for large industry. This does not mean that science should stop its work on anti-pollution devices, but more trees would certainly ease the problem. Of course, if a planet could harness solar energy, many of its pollution problems would be automatically solved.

Upon hearing this, Jason expressed his concern about the people who lived in city apartments, but Sebastian found a solution for that also. "If you cannot have anti-pollution outside, you bring it inside. Anyone can have flowers, green leafy plants, and small decorative trees inside homes and apartments. These would possibly provide inside environmental protection in a similar manner as a tree does outdoors."

Sebastian's solution pleased everyone and they looked forward to the time when they could pass this information on to Earth.

When the sun rose the next day, the Htrae family again hurried to the woods, the home of Brother Arbo. His "Harrumph" seemed a bit softer. On the other hand, the great tree had just met the Starians and he certainly did not want them to know that he was beginning to like them.

After everyone settled down and turned his or her attention to the great tree, Brother Arbo began. "Yesterday we talked about the energy field that exists around all things. You learned that trees serve as important anti-pollution devices because of the energy they produce. If too many are cut down and none planted to replace them, eventually the pollution from the greater cities moves into smaller cities, then into villages. After a time, pollution even penetrates the topsoil of a planet and all life is affected. People bodies become tired, sleepy and depressed, yet no one realizes they are actually being poisoned."

The tree teacher paused for a few moments, and then added, "Of course, trees do not work alone. All life is dependent on all other growing things."

Upon hearing this, Jason, who had started to compose the "Music of the Trees" thought that he had perhaps made an interesting discovery during his writing and decided to ask Brother Arbo a question. "Brother Arbo, last night I started to write a song about you. Suddenly I began to feel more energetic. I realized my thoughts about trees were actually drawing their energy to me. Does this mean that people who think good thoughts about the weather and appreciates the beauty of nature will receive greater benefits than those who do not?"

Jason's recognition of this fact promptly drew another "Harrumph" from Brother Arbo.

Fortunately, the Starians were learning that their teacher's "Harrumph" and grumbles did not necessarily mean he was displeased, but concerned.

When Brother Arbo finally answered he said, "That is true, Jason. However, you must not waste a great deal of time thinking about me just to become more energetic. The human mind actually does much of this naturally. For instance, you cannot run with the wind without thinking about it. The primary problem is that people bodies seldom give enough attention to their surroundings to make this a natural process."

As he thought of this, Brother Arbo gave an agitated grumble.

The next few months with Brother Arbo passed quickly and the Starians learned to keep their windows open during the night, enabling the body with its land of little people to function better because it had no interference from the conscious mind — which was asleep. The cell-people carefully absorbed their needs from the fresh air blowing through the sleeping rooms from the great forest. Later, these supplies were removed from the cell storehouses in order to repair and regenerate the people bodies as necessary. Naturally, Gusty was always present during such work to insure that it was done properly.

The Starians were also careful to plant flowers around their homes for pollination by the bees, which their friend, Gusty then took to all parts of the planet. Brother Arbo had explained that this too was a very important biological function. They also only took the timber for their homes from the densely wooded areas. This way they did not damage the forest, but actually helped to thin it. In turn, this made it possible for other trees to grow bigger and larger. When any new home was finished, the Starians enthusiastically planted little Brother Arbos around it. This replaced the trees they used and kept their planet beautiful, as well as ecologically balanced.

In time, the forest became larger due to having been carefully thinned; yet the people of Htrae had taken all the wood they needed for building. By now, Brother Arbo had become accustomed to the happy sound of people running to and fro as they built their homes and cities. Eventually it was not only the senior Starians, who came to admire him, but also all the other Starians and their children. Sometimes the great tree would look down and see the little ones looking up at him in great awe. When this occurred, his knothole heart would fill up with so much love he could hardly contain it. Other times Brother Arbo gently sheltered the children from the icy winds and falling rain. Of course his "harrumphs" still continued, but they were meant to preserve his image as the "Great Tree" rather than to complain.

Although the Starians were not actually aware of it, their ideas were reaching Earth in quite an unusual manner. It so happened, that far away in a distant city on Earth there were a few people who met regularly to discuss the possibilities of life beyond their planet. Sometimes they would look through telescopes for signs of advanced civilizations, and other times they would close their eyes and communicate with Lord of the Stars.

One night one of the members of this group, a freelance writer, saw a bright object float across his mind, which looked like a large crystal. Then he saw strange little creatures with, what looked like space helmets, wiry legs, a great solar nebulae and a most remarkable tree.

Hardly able to contain his excitement, Kenneth immediately began to share his adventure with others in the group, saying, "There could be life beyond Earth after all. A ball of light just passed through my mind and suddenly I perceived a way to help man with the pollution problem. It has something to do with trees, flowers, and grass. I can't explain it yet, but I will try to make some notes. Perhaps, as I write, everything will then become clear."

"Can't you tell us anything more about your experience?" someone asked with great curiosity.

"It all happened so fast," the writer replied. "I am not exactly certain about everything that passed through my inner vision. It seemed to have something to do with a very unusual planet whose inhabitants are called Starians. From what I understood, their planet was created by the Lord of the Stars for the express reason of helping Earth graduate from human to divine."

For a moment Kenneth stopped speaking and looked out the window toward the sky wondering, "Is it possible that I have somehow contacted a planet of higher intelligence somewhere in the galaxy?"

"Possible," Kenneth thought, "but not probable." He was silent for a few more moments more. Finally he shook his head, "Starians — who ever heard of Starians?"

CHAPTER X

Moon Magic

Since the dawn of creation, moons have existed as glowing satellites around mother planets. There has always been speculation concerning their formation, although most scientists believe they either originated from the great asteroid belt, which now rests between Mars and Jupiter, or that they are fragmented particles which became separated during original land mass solidification. How moons were formed, however, is perhaps not quiet as important to human bodies as their effect. Certainly the Starians were very interested in these strange phenomena.

As soon as Sebastian and the others noticed that the moon appeared to affect on the tides of the sea, and that a ring of haze often appeared around it prior a storm, their curiosity could not be restrained. They wondered if the moon might not affect other things also. Unfortunately, finding an answer to these questions caused a bit of a dilemma, for there were as yet no books on the subject. Finally, the Starians decided to send a thought message to Ambassador Marius, asking him to come.

This time the Ambassador was not able to visit with the Starians immediately, but he sent a message that he would come as soon as he could. He explained that he was tied up for a brief time with some interplanetary peace talks between two civilizations in a far distant galaxy that had been at war for many years.

While the Starians waited for Ambassador Marius' arrival, they decided to occupy themselves with other matters. There was always much to do on their planet, for a great deal of building was still going on. By this time, of course, the planet was occupied by millions of Starians and there were cities, cultural centers and homes to build, as well as transportation problems to resolve. Nevertheless, occasionally, Sally, Jason, Cedric and the rest still talked about life as it once was in the beginning of Htrae. Other times they talked about the future, for they knew it would soon be time for them to put *Operation Earth Angel* into effect. The thought of fulfilling their destiny pleased them a great deal.

When Ambassador Marius was free to join the Starians; they could hardly contain their curiosity about the moon. The Ambassador could see that they seemed to be excited over something and once everyone had settled down in the classroom, he asked, "Now what matter is so important to you that you have called me?"

Sebastian replied with a smile, "I suppose we do get somewhat enthusiastic about things. True, we probably could have asked our other teachers, but the subject did not seem quite appropriate. Sir Cellular teaches cell life, Mother Htrae teaches planetary things and Professor Biogenics teaches biochemistry. At the moment, however, we want to know more about the moon. All of us have noticed that it has a certain effect on our planet, such as the ocean tides. I feel we are still missing something that might be very important."

Ambassador Marius looked at Sebastian with a hint of amusement in his eyes. "Ah! Have you not discovered the secret of discovery yet Sebastian?"

The look in Ambassador Marius' eyes did not go unnoticed by Sebastian, but the secret of discovery intrigued him, "I suppose I haven't," he replied, "had I, I would understand what you are saying. Therefore, I must ask, what is it the secret of discovery anyway?"

"The secret of discovery is one's ability to ferret the cause of anything and everything at anytime," the Ambassador replied.

With this announcement, all of the Starians blinked their eyes and stared at Ambassador Marius. At the same time, they thought it would be pretty wonderful if they could really do what he said. However, that hardly seemed possible.

"I see that you doubt that you can really do this," the Ambassador stated. "Remember, I was once in a human body and yet I can find the cause of anything and everything at anytime. Therefore, you must be able to do the same thing. Perhaps it is because you do not know that you can.

"You see, thought travels faster than the speed of light and unites with its target, meaning that when one thinks of something they automatically become linked with the object of their thoughts. If the thinker is not obsessed by possessing the object, such as wanting it, but rather sends the mind to probe its nature, then the object has no recourse but to reveal its' self. As you learned from cloud zapping, the molecular structure of any one thing is less than the power of the mind, and must surrender to a greater will.

"Thus, all you have to do to learn the mysteries of the moon is to think about it." Ambassador Marius continued, "This is called the science of observation, although it is better known throughout the galaxies by the great wisdoms, as contemplation. This practice, when done properly, makes it possible for anyone to become knowledgeable in the underlying cause of any specific thing.

"Actually, all of the original books on religion, science, and philosophy have been created through observation. Of course, as with all things, observation is not without its weakness. Unfortunately, unwritten facts are only as good as the understanding of those who write them. For this reason there often appears to be a constant kaleidoscope of contradictions. However, the longer a person studies some particular subject the more knowledgeable he or she becomes."

By this time Sally, who was listening very intently, had a question. "Do you mean that we really don't have to read any books at all, because the consciousness of everything that has been written already exist in both the visible and invisible worlds at all times?"

"That is correct, Sally," Ambassador Marius replied. "Nevertheless, there is still one obstacle to this reasoning. If there were no books, then the doorway to higher learning could be hindered. Sometimes it takes someone else to make us aware of the exciting worlds we have not yet discovered. After all, we cannot expect to be involved in all things at once. To safe guard against this possibility, one must study only the writings of great wisdoms. That is if they desire to become wise."

"It would appear then," Sebastian, commented, "that we are back to that old subject, we become what we think. If we read inferior books, our minds cannot reach our highest potential."

"Well spoken, Sebastian," the inner-stellar teacher responded. "At the same time, one must not forget that some very great adventures are waiting in the world of new discoveries. All things from rocks to people are living organisms which contain the memory patterns of their existence."

Ambassador Marius paused for a minute before adding, "Although I could teach you many things about the moon, I do not believe I will do so, at least not at this time. First I would rather that you practice the science of contemplation and see what you can discover on your own. It will present a whole new world of exploration, one that I believe you will enjoy immensely. You will find that the moon is not only a living thing, but it has quite a history. I'm afraid it is a bit mischievous at times."

As soon as he had said this, the Ambassador instantly dematerialized.

"I would like to be able to do that," Cedric commented as he looked at the empty spot where the teacher had been standing, but a second before.

Later that evening, Cedric looked out of his window at the stars, his gaze moving over the heavens. When he saw the new moon bathing the land in shimmering light, he thought, "How beautiful and peaceful everything is at night."

Although Cedric wished that he could paint the beauty exactly as he now saw it, he knew that a painting could never be anything but a shadowed reflection the real thing.

With a measure of longing, the artist surveyed the hushed stillness. Slowly a feeling of great peace surrounded him, and he realized that peace and joy were somewhat like musical notes of a piano. He now believed that the Lord of the Stars must contain millions of vibratory frequencies within him. If so, then a human could play any tune they wished, such as happiness or sadness.

Cedric found the possibility of such a cosmic keyboard somewhat fascinating, for it meant that happiness could be achieved by touching the cosmic piano's joy key, comprised of the happy collective thoughts of all people. Unhappiness would only occur only if someone failed to understand the nature of the cosmic keyboard well and played a sad key.

As Cedric drifted into the silent world of dreams, he heard the voice of the Lord of the Stars. "Yes, Cedric, within me is indeed a great keyboard of vibrations, and each soul must learn to play it well if they are to achieve mastery over the world of matter. Nonetheless, I promise that you and all the other Starians will indeed master these cosmic vibratory frequencies one day, as will Earth. Wait and see."

The next morning when Cedric awakened, a sense of peace and knowing remained, and the words of Lord of the Stars still echoed in his memory. Later, when he told the others of his experience, they listened intently.

For a moment Sebastian touched the antennae on top of his head, then he spoke saying, "You know I believe that mastery of the cosmic keyboard and visiting other worlds are somehow related. When you stop to think about it, each of us has actually played a different note every time we created a new form.

"Obviously everything in the universe is alive and every life form vibrates at a frequency that makes it what it is, including us. Just as Jason has perfected his music, our forms have also been refined with each passing cycle of progression. It is therefore logical to assume that we will one day outgrow our people bodies and go on to other worlds. However, it also appears that we must learn to play the notes of our people bodies well before we can move on."

Sebastian fell silent for a moment, as though he was mulling over a thought, and then he continued, "Perhaps it is best that we do not to get too involved in this interesting puzzle right now, or we may not get our daily planetary work completed. Remember, Brother Arbo taught us that a number of the great wisdoms meditated on Mother Nature in the morning and Lord of the Stars in the evening."

"I know why they did that," interjected Joan. "Nature is always awake and very active in the morning. Sometimes, if I sit around thinking for a long time in the morning, I feel lazy and have difficulty beginning my work. It is almost as though I no longer vibrate harmoniously with other life on the planet. Since everything becomes active when the sun rises, I suppose we should be active also."

Webster nodded in agreement and made a suggestion that they get together in the evening for some evening meditation. "Perhaps we will be fortunate enough to capture a bit of moon magic like Cedric." He smiled.

About this time the Starians saw Franklin approaching them. His clothes were torn and he was covered with black soot from head to foot.

Greatly concerned by his disheveled appearance, Sally cried out, "Oh, Franklin! What happened to you?"

Franklin seemed somewhat in a daze. "I am not at all sure what went wrong, Sally," he replied. "Apparently I managed to fall down Sebastian's chimney. I had taken my most recent flying machine to the roof and I was just getting ready to take off when Old Gusty gave me a helpful shove. The airplane lifted high into the air, flew over Sebastian's roof, and landed in that tree over there without me. I believe I must have been upside down when I fell, though the details are pretty foggy."

Franklin looked sadly at the top of the tree and then at the ground where the plane lay in pieces. "Perhaps it is time to give up flying and concentrate on electricity instead."

The Lord of the Stars, who had witnessed Franklin's debacle, was so amused that he almost stopped creating new worlds. Ambassador Marius was also amused, but he knew that the Lord of the Stars enjoyed sharing the adventures of his children on all planets. Mentally the Ambassador reached out with his consciousness to touched bases with the ruler of the universe, "I suppose, my Lord, that Franklin's effort to fly is the source of your entertainment"

"Indeed so, Ambassador Marius," the ruler over the universe replied. "Franklin just fell down a chimney during his flying lesson. Now that is no easy task! You know, it requires flying upside down."

The Ambassador became quite serious. "Perhaps I should look into the matter, because I believe you once said that Franklin is not destined to invent flying."

"Well, at least not airplanes," the Lord of the Stars replied, "but I did help Gusty give him a bit of a push anyway, just to encourage him. Franklin has been trying so hard. Of course you are quite right; he is not destined to invent the flying machine. Hopefully, he will soon become more interested in harnessing solar energy, although you may have to prod him a bit. It is hard for some humans to give up their desires, even when their interests are not in harmony with their destiny."

For a moment the Lord of the Stars was silent and then he said, "Ambassador Marius, I have an idea. I believe I will give Franklin a surprise trip to the moon in the near future. I trust his landing will be somewhat softer,"

Following these words, the Lord of the Stars took a deep breath and finished his observation, pleased that the flying lesson was concluded so that creation could continue.

Ambassador Marius was a bit puzzled over the comment about giving Franklin a flying trip to the moon, but he set about his other affairs knowing that the Lord of the Stars would reveal the mystery in good time. After millions of years serving as the Lord's ambassador, Ambassador Marius knew that the Lord of the Stars often worked in mysterious ways.

That same evening, just as the sun was setting, Webster, Franklin, Cedric, Sebastian and Jason prepared for dinner. After washing carefully, they entered the large room where the evening meals were generally served. Sally, who had become the official cook, greeted everyone happily.

"I have prepared a special dinner tonight which I hope everyone will enjoy." She walked over to Franklin and touched his cheek. "I thought perhaps something special would make you feel better about your airplanes, Franklin."

"Good food, served with love, is often the best antidote for a day of tribulations, Sally," Franklin said, trying to make his forlorn smile a bit more cheerful.

After the last bite of dinner had been savored, Jason played the piano and the others stood around and sang. By now Jason's music expressed the movement of the rivers, the whispering of the trees, and the falling rain. His songs always revealed the story of creation, the travels of the wind, and love for Lord of the Stars. These were happy times, for the group knew that their thoughts of the Cosmic Father were always received and that their music united them as one family with all of the planets in the universe.

Time passed swiftly as the Starians sang and almost before they knew it, it was time for meditation. Although they had meditated on many things, they never concentrated on each other. They knew that to do so could pass any unhappiness in them on to the others. Yet, they also knew that to meditate on the Lord of the Stars, or on the great wonders throughout the universe, would help them to give birth to the greatness within themselves. Tonight they decided to visit the moon, and as the magic hour approached for their thought journey to the moon they formed their chairs in a circle. This was to symbolize the Lord of the Stars' eternal wisdom without end.

First, everyone closed their eyes and directed love to the whole planet. This helped them to turn any bad thoughts emanating from the people bodies of their planet into good thoughts. At the same time, this also helped protect them from receiving the bad thoughts of others. After the Starians had completed enveloping their planet with their love, they closed their eyes and began to visualize the moon in the dark place behind the forehead.

After a short time, a sense of peace began to enfold each member of the circle, just as it had Cedric the night before. However, as this state of consciousness engulfed Franklin he became a star, and his soul soared upward to the moon. No longer did he feel human, but pure spirit. As Franklin traveled through the night sky into the vast Universe he was no longer aware of his people body or even a light body, yet he still sensed he was Franklin. In seconds his soul landed on the rocky surface of the moon. In a distance the inventor saw Htrae gleaming like a brilliant sapphire.

At the same time he also saw another planet. It was all green and blue, and in a distance appeared somewhat like a small emerald. Franklin knew that it was Earth.

Standing on the moon and overlooking the heavens with an expanded vision of pure spirit, Franklin realized that he loved all of the planets in the vast universe. However, there was a very special feeling for the green and blue planet spinning in the distance. "Just a little longer, Earth," he said, "we are trying to hurry so that we might help you."

Suddenly Franklin felt a gentle tug and he was pulled rapidly back into his people body.

When everyone had finished meditating and opened their eyes, Franklin made a startling announcement. "I shall cease my efforts to invent a flying machine. From now on my attention shall be directed toward harnessing solar energy."

"But Franklin," Sally exclaimed, "You have tried so hard to create a flying machine. Really, all of us have wanted you to succeed."

"Sally, I did succeed in a rather unusual way. My soul has flown far beyond the capability of airplanes and I no longer feel a need for a physical flying machine. Remember, we are far more than Starians. Although we know that our real selves are not the various forms we have worn throughout the growth of our planet, and that we become what we think, we almost forgot that our real self is actually a part of the Lord of the Stars. This true self is free of all forms. Therefore, anyone can fly anywhere. All they have to do is to cease being anything other than their real self. It's easy, once you accept it."

Then Franklin told them about his trip to the moon and the beauty of the planet Earth.

"Until we arrive, Earth must harness solar energy in order to continue the survival of human life," Franklin said." Somehow I know there is someone like me on Earth who needs my knowledge, and I must see that this knowledge is passed on some way. It is obvious to me now; this is what I am supposed to do. No wonder flying never really worked out well, for we must fulfill our real purpose.

Everyone looked at Franklin with deep understanding. Each one of the Starians had also been pondering upon exactly the role each of them was destined to play in *Operation Earth Angel*. It was Joan who spoke up and expressed the sentiment that was in all their hearts, "Oh! Franklin, that is wonderful. When you think about it, harnessing solar energy is kind of like flying, but I think better. After all an airplane will only overcome the pull of gravity, but harnessing the sun reaches far beyond that. What a wonderful challenge."

When Franklin heard these words, he looked at Joan with great tenderness, "What a kind thing to say Joan. Somehow you have turned destiny into life's great adventure."

Shaking his head from side-to-side in a thoughtful manner, Franklin, half speaking to the group and half speaking to himself said; "No, I shall not mind leaving my interest in flying behind, and I do look forward to harnessing solar energy. At the same time I must say, it is amazing how much trouble one can get into when one does not follow their purpose."

Upon hearing this, all of the Starians laughed and nodded their heads in agreement. Then Webster spoke up, "We noticed that the moon affects the tides of the sea as it orbits around Htrae. Therefore, because Sir Cellular taught us that people bodies are mostly water, it seems apparent that people bodies are also connected to the ocean by common vibration. By this I mean the water in the bodies connects with the water in the ocean. This, of course, could explain why the moon so often affects people."

"If that is true," replied Sebastian, "then the pull of the moon's gravity would also affect any point of a planet nearest to it. In other words, it probably affects our location on Htrae more at one time than another."

"That seems very logical Sebastian. Some of my own research has indicated that the moon has an influence over both crops and the birth of children," Joan added. "Sometimes it also seems to cause obvious changes in a human's mental activity, but I have never really heard a good explanation for this peculiar relationship."

"We can only assume in this case Joan, that the moon, having its own gravity field around it, affects the gravity pull of any nearby planet," answered Sebastian. "In other words, life on any given planet, including Htrae, is held to the planet's surface by its gravity. Now along comes the moon and affects the flow of the planet's gravity by its own gravitational pull. This pull on any planet by a moon would probably create something like a tug-of-war. Therefore, it would affect not only a planet, but also its people. The more sensitive, or higher evolved a soul is, the more sensitive it would be,"

"Sebastian, you are amazing! You seem to have the uncanny ability to find any answer," Webster applauded. "I don't see how any of us could get along without you."

Sebastian merely shrugged his shoulders and smiled. "Remember that you can indeed do without me, for the potential to understand all things lives within everyone. But tell me, Franklin, did you see any life forms while you were on the moon?"

"While I did not sense beings of any kind, that does not mean there were none. You must realize my visit was quite brief," Franklin replied. "Actually, any life form more evolved than that of a human would probably not be visible to people eyes because it would be vibrating too rapidly. Oddly enough, advanced life would probably be quite invisible to most of those in people bodies."

Next, Webster added his discoveries concerning the moon. "If the moon is also a form of consciousness, or intelligence, all planets in the galaxies must consist of intelligence. Each would then have its effect on any nearby planet, just as the moon has. This is probably how the ancient science of astronomy was developed. Wise men, realizing there was both motion and consciousness of various planets, started to plot their influences on other planetary life. The closer one planet is to another, the greater the effect."

Sebastian, who had been concentrating quite intently, interjected, "It is entirely possible that our friend the moon is responsible for the development of astronomy. As the closest landmass to our planet, as well as to Earth, it can be studied more easily and its effects observed at the same time. From the moon, the ancient ones would have realized that all planets in the solar system, or even the universe, affect one another."

For a moment Sebastian stopped speaking. Then he added, "It is really quite fascinating. You know, Astronomy could actually become a lifetime study."

By this time Cedric also had something to say about Moon Magic, "Sebastian, if we looked at the moon from your perspective we could say that the planets form a great cosmic symphony. Because everything is a part of one great plan, it therefore becomes one great sound.

"In the scheme of cosmic music, the moons could be seen as the black keys on a piano creating sharps and flats. Of course, a sour note would exist any time a planet was separated from its true nature. Such a planet would be one that is involved in wars and hatred. Like an off-key piano, an inharmonious planet would need to be tuned because it, in turn, affects an entire solar system. Perhaps this doesn't really have a great deal to do with moon magic, but these various realizations we are experiencing seems to have started with the moon."

"That is an excellent insight, Cedric," Sebastian added. "Apparently the Lord of the Stars keeps each planet tuned through the unhappiness and sorrow everyone experiences when they are disobedient to his ways. It is not that he intends to punish, but more that each person creates their own punishment so that they can learn their unlearned lessons. It does place quite a responsibility on everyone, doesn't it?"

Sebastian then turned to Joan and asked, "Did a bit of moon magic touch you also?"

"Oh yes, for I heard that which is called the 'Music of the Spheres'. It must be that the great music created by composers everywhere becomes delicate sound vibrations that live forever. As I sought the moon, my mind became so quiet I found it possible to tune into those vibrations." Joan replied. "I think that we would all have to agree; when people become aware of their lack of any real limitation, they can hear this great music without radio or television. To me, it was like the music of the angels."

Whenever Sally contemplated on a new truth and reached some new conclusion, she always became very excited. Now, in her exuberance, her words quickly tumbled out one after another. Joyously she announced, "This means that the talent of all great painters everywhere is also in the storehouse of cosmic consciousness, as well as the knowledge of all philosophy and science. Do you suppose that this is what Ambassador Marius was trying to tell us; we can learn anything, anywhere at anytime because we are truly unlimited!"

In that moment Sally broke through her Starian reality to experience her true unlimited self. "Now I understand what you meant, Franklin, when you said we are more than Starians," she said with awe.

Shortly after Sally ceased speaking, the group made the decision to end their Circle of Wisdom and depart for their own homes. As Sebastian walked along the path toward his house with his hands in his pockets, he was in deep thought. Glancing upward and looking at the moon, he spoke quietly, "Lord of the Stars, how could anyone ever really doubt that you exist, or that you have a great plan for all creation and sustain the universe?"

Next, what Sebastian saw then made him rub his eyes. Was it a trick of his imagination, or did the moon actually wink at him?

CHAPTER XI

The Elsewhere Land

The brilliant sun which had shone on Htrae throughout the day now dropped behind the mountain range at the edge of the great forest. For a brief time the sky glowed with softening shades of red, orange, and violet, and then these colors also faded into the opaque night. By this time the Starians were snug in their beds, and their souls had withdrawn from their people bodies to enjoy the period known as sleep.

Now that the Htrae family had retired for the night, the Lord of the Stars drew a deep breath. Because things were quiet, he decided that a conference with Ambassador Marius about the forthcoming mission of the Starians was in order. It would soon be time to begin final preparations for *Operation Earth Angel*, but the Lord felt that there were a few details that should be considered first.

As soon Ambassador Marius received the summons from the Lord of the Stars he hastened quickly to the conference. "You called my Lord?" the Ambassador asked.

"Yes indeed Ambassador," the Lord answered. "I must say that it is always good to visit with you. I called, however, because I do not believe it will be long before the Starians can fulfill *Operation Earth Angel*. Since you are overseeing their progress I wanted to discuss the matter with you. While I am aware of the overall progress of the Htrae family, I have left the more intricate matters of their progression in your hands. I would feel it would be quite helpful if I could hear your opinion."

Ambassador nodded his head before speaking, and then he replied, "The Starians have progressed nicely and maintained their cosmic awareness, even in people bodies. Nonetheless, I believe that they will each need one more journey to the Elsewhere Land before they are fully prepared to assume the graduation of Earth. Sebastian and the others senior Starians have accomplished a great deal this life, but their people bodies are wearing out again. I believe another season of soul experience will further enhance the effectiveness of their mission."

"What about Earth?" the Lord asked. "Is it in any real danger yet?"

"Although it is still moving closer to the asteroid belt each day my Lord, I believe there will be sufficient time for the Starians to prepare a bit more before trying to fulfill their mission. I am confident that we have sufficient time."

"All right Ambassador, but please keep me posted," the Lord of the Stars requested. Then, almost as an aftermath he added, "You know, I am looking forward to Earth's graduation very much. My, the Earthlings do have some remarkable surprises in store for them. Won't they be amazed to find that most things are not actually as they seem?"

The Ambassador smiled when he heard the Lord allude to the surprises ahead for Earth. Then he bowed and took his leave.

Later, as the Lord of the Stars went about his work of creation, he thought about the birth of Htrae and the family of little golden souls. Before long they would become pure white light and fulfill their mission to save Earth. "How wonderful it will be to welcome Earth into their next phase of soul progression," the Lord mused. "If they only knew what awaited them, but of course that is a surprise. "

Not long after the conference between the Lord of the Stars and Ambassador Marius, Franklin, who was lying on his bed beneath the stars, awakened and realized that he was becoming more and more tired with each passing day. He knew that his aging people body did not allow him to think as well anymore, and that his work seemed to be getting harder to accomplish. Sometimes he even forgot to complete his experiments. It wasn't that the millions of years spent in building Htrae hadn't made him greater; it was simply that his people bodies wore out from time-to-time.

Wearily Franklin shook his head. He saw that he must yet make another trip to the Elsewhere Land before he could complete his work. He regretted that he had not yet been able to finish harnessing solar energy, primarily because he knew that Earth needed it so badly.

Even as Franklin thought about his work, he began to experience the very peaceful feeling that always came when the journey to the Elsewhere Land was about to begin. He felt he, as the soul, begin to withdraw from his people body and as he withdrew, the body became colder and no longer movable. Soon, he floated free of the aging form. As he did so, he heard the voice of an old friend.

"Greetings once again, Franklin, how are you this fine evening?"

The voice was that of Master Ether, who appeared as a mass

of vibrating purple light and possessed eyes of sparkling gold. Although Master Ether was pure light, he always demonstrated a remarkable adaptation to all worlds by taking on whatever form was acceptable to those he visited. These various forms were always created from the ether substance of unseen worlds, just as human bodies were made from the substances of the physical worlds. At the same time, his golden eye beams made it possible for him to travel in the many worlds beyond the physical universe. Of course, he was well known to the Starians, who had met him on other journeys, and they loved him a great deal, both as their guide and their teacher.

"Why, hello, Master Ether! It's truly a pleasure to see you again!" Franklin answered. "I must say, it really feels quite good to be free of my aging people body. Nevertheless, I wish I could have completed my experiments first. Sometimes it seems that a single life just doesn't contain enough time."

"Come, come, Franklin," Master Ether said kindly. "Remember, time is eternal and that the journey in a people body is but an experience in the perfection of the soul. Why, there have been times during the past few years that you forgot to put on your socks. If we allowed this sort of thing to continue, you might eventually forget your own name and the great work you set out to do."

"Hmmm, I suppose you are right, as always. I suppose also, that I will just have to make the best of it." Franklin sighed. "By the way, I believe Sally, Sebastian and Cedric are here someplace. I have missed them very much since they left earth, and I look forward to seeing them again. Life is simply not same when they are not there. We certainly had some wonderful adventures."

"Well, let me see." Master Ether stopped for a moment in order to scan the unseen world through the heightened senses of a semi-light, semi-material body. "Um-m-m! You are quite right; I do see that your friends are here. Sally is teaching psychology to a group of Starians who failed to develop sufficient compassion during their last life. This will give the group a chance to do better next time."

"That does sound like Sally, but what about Sebastian and Cedric?" Franklin asked.

"It will probably be no surprise to you, Cedric is still painting. Apparently, he is teaching a bit of painting to a few his former students, also now in the Elsewhere Land. Other times, however, he works at transferring his consciousness into some of his admirers still in people bodies. This, of course, helps them become better artists.

"That reminds me Franklin," Master Ether turned to look at Franklin with his deep penetrating golden eyes, "what are you planning to do this trip?"

"I haven't really had time to seriously think about it," Franklin replied. "I fear that my departure from earth was somewhat unexpected, for I woke up from a deep sleep and knew that I would have to leave.

"You mentioned Cedric and the power of thought transference, however, and I am fascinated over this potential. Surely there must be someone on Earth who is seeking to harness solar energy and I could pass on my knowledge to him." That way I would lose no time and my part in *Operation Earth Angel* could continue."

Pausing to make certain that his plan would be effective before speaking, Franklin then turned to Master Ether and said, "I believe I would like permission to go into the inner penetrating ether substance of Earth and help someone who is working on solar energy through the transference of consciousness. I have made many interesting discoveries in the past years that could be of great help. In turn, the knowledge of whatever we achieved there would return with me when I re-enter another people body."

Master Ether considered this a few moments before replying.

Then he spoke, saying, "I am certain I can arrange for you to do that. However, first it is time to review your life. After that I will take you to visit your friends.

"By the way," the Master of the Elsewhere Land added, "some of your other acquaintances will be along shortly. Jason has some students anxiously awaiting him here and Joan is getting much too old for the hardships of her extensive lecture tours. Of course, there is Webster, who reads and writes nearly every waking moment. He has failing eyesight. Thus, I will be meeting each of them again very soon."

"The continuity of life never ceases to amaze me," Franklin replied. "It goes on and on forever, even far beyond the existence of human bodies. Sometimes I wonder why we strive so hard during people lives to do the seemingly impossible when we do live forever. At the same time, I realize it is our true nature to do this, because we are part of a plan greater ourselves."

"That is quite right, Franklin. People always believe these worlds to be Heaven, rather than an extension of life. It takes a while to understand that higher worlds cannot be reached until people lessons are learned properly."

Master Ether shook his head. "To live on the Planet of the Angels, people must develop angel-like qualities while in people bodies. As you know, some have managed to do this."

By now, Master Ether and Franklin had arrived in the lower ethers where the past is reviewed. Although many believed that this is a period of judgment where man is punished for his bad deeds, Franklin knew that this was not a true picture. He had been to the Elsewhere Land other times, and understood that review allowed the soul to view its accomplishments, as well as its mistakes. In turn, this better prepared the soul to assume another people body and have a better life.

First, the review determined exactly which part of the unseen world was right for each person, because different ideology still separated souls in the ether world just as it caused separation on the people planets. Secondly, the review helped to determine the circumstances to be experienced during the soul's next journey into matter. Little would be accomplished if a soul could always live exactly as he or she chose. The Great Plan of the Lord of the Stars, on the other hand, assured the constant progression to every soul in the universe. The universe was structured in such a way as to insure that the remarkable Law of Cause and Effect bound each life form. This guaranteed that the unlearned lessons would be learned.

As Franklin sat down in his favorite meditation position, scenes from the soul record pertaining to his life began its journey through his mind. It was somewhat like watching a motion picture, but the pictures were reviewed from within rather than upon a movie screen. He watched himself being born as an infant, growing to maturity, and aging into an old man. He was surprised to find he hadn't accomplished nearly as much as he thought he had, particularly during his last years. Yet, when he saw the homes of Htrae filled with warmth and light because he had discovered a way to harness electricity he knew then that it had been a good life. Like most souls, however, he planned to do even better the next time.

At last the review was finished and Franklin got up to join Master Ether, who was waiting to take him through the higher regions of the unseen world. First, however, the Master decided to take Franklin into the lower realms in order to deepen his understanding of life after death. Therefore their first stop occurred in the realm where those dwelled who had made very serious mistakes in life. Next, the two of them journeyed through the land of the arrogant, selfish, and unloving souls who had made others unhappy. This was quickly followed by the realm of the good, whose violations of natural and cosmic law were less severe, but whose eyes were still blinded by the world of matter.

As Franklin observed these things, he noticed at each level his body became lighter. "Here in Elsewhere Land there seems to be a suitable plane for each and every one," he thought.

Even as he had these thoughts, Franklin also realized these higher worlds were still only a reflection of Lord of the Stars, yet more perfect than planets sustaining people bodies.

At last, Master Ether and Franklin came to a stop. Master Ether turned to Franklin and said, "Franklin, you actually did very well during your last life and have reached the realm of the golden ones. Before much more time has passed, you will become divine and graduate from the cycles of earthly necessity. Then, of course, you will become pure white light and work from the Angelic Kingdom."

Master Ether paused for a moment before continuing. "Now I must leave you, but I doubt I shall be missed. I see some of your friends coming toward us and you will have a great deal to talk about. While you visit with them, I will make the necessary arrangements for your work on the inner planes of Earth."

With this Master Ether instantly disappeared, for people traveled by thought in the Elsewhere Land. As soon as a place is visualized, one was immediately there. Franklin watched the disappearing Master and then turned to see a soft light edged with gold approaching him. In the light's center stood one of his old acquaintances. "Sebastian!" Franklin clasped his friend warmly. "I have missed you so on Htrae."

"It is very good to see you again also, Franklin," Sebastian replied. Looking fondly at his old friend, he inquired about their other long time acquaintances on Htrae. "I would like to hear all the news about our planet, and then I must show you some of the work I am doing." For a moment he grew silent. "It seems that I am to complete my planetary work during the next life, so I must prepare well."

"Sebastian, I am so delighted to hear that, but it does not really surprise me." Pausing, Franklin looked out over the far-reaching cosmos where the destiny of each soul and each planet is carefully etched. For a moment it seemed that he saw an old dead tree standing deep in the North Woods, and around it the soul form of six Starians, as well a beautiful angelic being. Turning back to Sebastian with happiness he said, "In fact, old friend, I am confident we will all be with you then. Apparently, the people cycle on our planet is almost finished."

As they walked along, Cedric and Sally joined Sebastian and Franklin. After giving Franklin a warm welcome they inquired about his work, for they were greatly interested in the progress of Franklin's work on solar energy. They expressed their condolences when they learned that the task had not been completed, for everyone knew how hard Franklin worked.

The discussion on electricity and solar energy was put aside, and Franklin mentioned that Master Ether had told him Webster, Joan and Jason was soon to join them. This pleased the others, for life in the elsewhere land was filled with greater love than on people planets, and Sebastian, Cedric and Sally still missed their friends.

After spending considerable time together catching up of each other's activities, Sebastian turned to Franklin with regret and said, "Franklin, I must leave you for a while. There is a great deal of work to do here. My students are already assembled in the classroom and waiting for me to come and teach ancient wisdom." Pausing, he reached for Franklin's hand and clasped it. "I'll meet with you again soon."

The other Starians smiled at Sebastian's parting figure, and soon they left also to continue with their own individual work.

As Franklin watched them go, he wondered why people sorrowed when someone died. Obviously those who were left behind missed a person who had moved beyond a people body, but they would always meet again if they truly wanted to. Life simply continued its evolution to a greater perfection, whether in the Elsewhere Land or in human form. Of course, it was more pleasant and harmonious in the worlds beyond the physical, but because of this, the progress of the soul was slower.

"Somehow," there is a great beauty to this movement of cosmic order" Franklin thought. "If all souls could only understand the great tides of planetary progression, they would never know sorrow again." He sighed, "One day, they will understand." In the meantime, there is much work to be done."

Suddenly, Master Ether materialized in front of Franklin and said kindly, "Permission has been granted for you to work with an Earth being on solar energy. My telepathic scan has picked up a human form named David March in the Bell Laboratories in California. David reminds me of you, as you were in your early days. At the moment, he is very discouraged, because he has long sought for a proper conduit for solar energy and each time he has met with failure. I believe you will be of great assistance to him."

In that instant a picture of Franklin's teacher, Sir Cellular, ruler of cell life, flashed in his mind, and Franklin chuckled. "Perhaps we should send Sir Cellular instead of me," he suggested. I see that David is addicted to donuts and black coffee.

Master Ether smiled. "It might not be a bad idea to call for Sir Cellular after all. But come, Franklin, let's go to California. Do you remember how to do this?"

"Well, I'm a bit rusty, but I believe I can manage it," Franklin answered. In the next instant they were standing in a large laboratory. In front of them sat a young man, elbows propped upon the table and his head between his hands. His face revealed the same weary frustration Franklin had felt so many times.

As Master Ether and Franklin studied the thought forms flowing out of David mind, they saw that another one of his experiments had just failed. Apparently it was the same problem which was plaguing scientific research on solar energy everywhere. So far, it had been impossible for anyone on earth to find a form of metal alloy that could both hold the energy and yet transmit it beyond a fixed location.

Master Ether looked at Franklin. "What do you think, Franklin?"

Franklin smiled. "If nothing else, I can at least guide David toward another metal, which contains a greater capacity to retain energy."

Ah then, I will leave you." On departing Master Ether touched Franklin's shoulder and said, "I will see you again before your return to Htrae. Remember, I am just a thought away if you need me. Good luck!"

With this final farewell, the Master was gone.

Franklin walked over to the table where David was working to look at the drawings lying on it. After he studied them thoroughly, he thought deeply about the different metals he had used in his own experiments. Holding a picture in his mind of an alloy that had proven more successful than any other, he began to transmit both the image and its properties carefully into David's mind.

Abruptly David raised his head, somewhat astounded that he felt more rested and less discouraged. "The problem has something to do with the particular metal I am using," he thought. "Apparently, I need to experiment with a metal having a greater solar storage potential, perhaps an alloy or even a crystal." As David muttered to himself, Franklin smiled. It was good to be back to work without the infirmity of an aging body.

Meanwhile, in the Elsewhere Land, Joan was just arriving. She and Jason had been out for an afternoon drive in the country when Jason fell asleep. Suddenly, when she looked down at her body, she saw that it was a much finer vibration than it had been just a few moments before. Quickly realizing that her lifestyle had suddenly changed, she sighed, "Oh well, the constant tours were becoming more difficult and I have needed a rest for a long time."

Joan shook herself, enjoying the new feeling of freedom.

Abruptly, a voice spoke to her. "Hello, Joan."

"Oh! Master Ether, how wonderful to see you again!" she exclaimed.

As they greeted each other, Joan remembered Jason, who had been in the accident with her, and hesitating, she said, "Before we leave, I must check on Jason. In the pleasure of seeing you, I had forgotten about him."

"I don't think you will have to worry about him long," Master Ether replied. "Jason is coming with us, but he is having a bit of difficulty getting out of his people body."

Soon they found themselves beside Jason, who was in a rather awkward position. He was half outside the body and half inside and temporarily resolving the situation by simply sitting. When he heard Joan's laughter, he turned to look at her. "You wouldn't think it was so funny if you were not certain whether you were leaving or staying," he commented.

"Please relax," Master Ether said. "You are coming with us, so we will wait for you." Then he sent a telepathic message to Sebastian, Cedric, and Sally to inform them that their two friends had arrived. Almost instantly the three of them appeared at the Master's elbow, smiling happily at the sight of their old friends.

When Jason, who was beginning to feel quite cheerful about the whole situation, saw Sally and the others beside him he began chatting merrily. Soon he felt a sense of weightlessness, and, at last, his soul slipped out of its people body. As the group walked along together, Jason looked around with a great deal of interest at the subtle ether world which interpenetrated the world he had just come from. Turning to the others, he said, "It is interesting to observe how the worlds of the invisible and visible are simply reflections of one another." The others nodded in agreement.

As the Starians continued on their journey, Jason saw some of his former students approaching. They showed a great deal of excitement and waved to him. Looking at them, Jason bowed, much as he had done when he had walked onto the stage in his people body. At the same time he commented to his friends, "It appears that our work in the human world is but an extension of this one also."

The period between the Elsewhere Land and the people world moved swiftly for the older members of the Htrae family. Soon each became aware that the time was drawing near to return to people bodies. One day, as the sun touched the sapphire waves of Htrae and Gusty sang his song through the trees of the glen, the cry of a newborn baby was heard. Mother Htrae paused from her gardening for a moment to listen. She recognized the cry well, as did Brother Arbo in the great North Woods. It came from the soul of one of the ancients of Htrae. It was Sebastian.

As Sebastian was born, the Lord of the Stars revealed to Mother Htrae that it would be Sebastian's last journey to the planet he loved so much. This time he would not only finish his mastery of the cosmic keyboard, but *Operation Earth Angel* would also be accomplished.

Mother Htrae smiled tenderly on hearing the news, but her attention was soon attracted to the cry of yet another newborn baby. Again, she paused in her work to listen. The cry of this infant sounded much nicer now than it had long ago when Jason had worn a dinosaur body, and sang his first song in squawks and gawks. "Yes," Mother Htrae thought, "the next few years promise to be most enjoyable, for the ancients will once again walk upon the land."

Far away on Planet Earth, Franklin looked down on David's white head. He had fallen asleep again. Franklin whispered, "You are getting old, David, and will soon pass into the unseen world of Earth." He touched his earth friend's shoulder gently, "I must leave you now, but we shall meet someday." He looked around the laboratory, remembering the years they had spent experimenting with alloys and crystals. He knew that it would not be long now before electrical energy, as it was now utilized, would be obsolete.

Within moments Franklin felt himself entering the circular vortex, much like a funnel. It was drawing him back into another people body. "Strange," he thought, "death is not really much different than birth. Death allows the soul freedom from its physical burdens and infirmities, but birth is a beginning, bringing with it forgetfulness of the past so that the soul can go on to learn new lessons."

Then another cry was soon heard floating on the wind of the Planet Htrae.

CHAPTER XII

Master Ether

*I*t was a dawn unlike any other. Nature rose from its sleep to display a brilliant array of violet, rose, gold, and brilliant orange. Much had changed since Htrae had been brought into being, and now the seventh and final epoch of Htrae's progression was about to begin. The time had come to set *Operation Earth Angel* in motion. Old Gusty carried this exciting news to the four corners of the universe, and a sense of expectancy hovered in the hearts of the other planets within Earth's solar system.

On Earth, a change had taken place. It seemed that as Htrae progressed so did Earth. People talked more about peace now, while ecologists sought better ways of preserving natural resources for future life. They still did not know, however, that they would become divine one day.

Perceiving that the time was nearing for the Starians to begin their mission, the Lord of the Stars called Ambassador Marius for consultation. As he had for billions of eons, the Lord transmitted a request to the Ambassador and asked that he join him.

Ambassador Marius, as always upon receiving such a request, arrived immediately. "I received your message my Lord, and to be called is always a delight. Whatever is your will is also my will."

"Ambassador, it is good that you have come. I have called you to discuss the divine birth of earth and the final phase of Starian preparation for *Operation Earth Angel*. I trust that everything is going as it should."

"Yes, my Lord. The senior members and leaders of Htrae have entered their final sojourn into human existence. They have almost perfected science, philosophy and the arts. Their leadership has established an exemplary pattern for the entire planet. As a result, most of the remaining Starians have full knowledge of their purpose, even to the youngest soul."

"Your news is as I suspected Ambassador Marius. How much more time do you think they will need?"

Ambassador Marius was silent for a moment before he spoke, considering the matter before him. Then he said, "First, we must pick a leader from amongst the senior members of Htrae. I believe this will be necessary in order that there be one spokesman to walk among the people bodies and prepare them for the final moment when Htrae will no longer exist. There are still some Starians who do not understand the full implication of the planet's final phase, and other that need more preparation. I must assume, of course, that the planet itself will cease to be, although the Starians, as well as Earth souls will exist forever."

"Quite right, Ambassador," the Lord replied. "Do you have someone in mind for this important role?"

"Yes, my Lord. There is little doubt but that Sebastian would be my first choice. He has always been a leader, as well as brilliant. He is currently Professor of Philosophy at Htrae's leading University, and greatly loved by everyone."

"Good. Then I trust that you will not only take over his final training Ambassador Marius, but you will begin immediately," replied the Lord of the Stars.

"Of course my Lord," the Ambassador replied, "However, do you mind my asking exactly how *Operation Earth Angel* is to enter its final phase?"

When the Lord of the Stars heard Ambassador's inquiry, he smiled. "Why, Ambassador, haven't you figured that out yet?"

Ambassador looked at the Lord and might have laughed, had important dignitaries allowed their senses rule over their emotions. "My Lord, your consciousness has given it away, and I perceive that it is as I suspected. My, Earth certainly does have a surprise in store. Your plan will indeed work perfectly. I will contact Master Ether to prepare Earth's angel robes."

The Lord of the Stars was silent, but as Ambassador Marius prepared to depart for Planet Htrae he felt the Lord's inner delight over creating such a great mystery.

Even as the Lord of the Stars and Ambassador Marius was discussing the divine birth of Htrae and Earth, Master Ether had also picked up on the vibratory waves emanating from the powerful creative thought force of the Lord of the Stars. Thus, he was not at all surprised when Ambassador Marius summoned him to counsel.

"Ambassador Marius," acknowledged Master Ether as he joined the Ambassador. "I see that we have two planets which will soon become divine, first Htrae and very shortly thereafter, Earth. This will be one of the greatest graduations in the history of the galaxies, and certainly one that a number of us have been preparing for. In fact I had the pleasure to meet with a group of the Starians not long ago in the Elsewhere Land. Now, however, I believe they have all returned to their home planet to prepare for the rendezvous with earth.

"Yes indeed, Master Ether, the senior Starians have returned to their planet. And, you are quite right, *Operation Earth Angel* will be most remarkable," replied the Ambassador. "In the meantime Htrae must be prepared for its final phase and this means training a Leader. I have not considered anyone other than you to take over this plan of the operation, for you have long headed the Angelic Kingdom and trained many great beings. At the moment I have a particular Starian in mind, Sebastian. He has been the primary leader of Htrae since the planet originated, although he has several close friends who have always been with him. They too are exceptional, but still – he had been a leader."

"I agree with you, Ambassador. I have met Sebastian numerous times in the Elsewhere Land and he is one of the most remarkable people souls I have ever met. Because he has always been such a good student, I doubt that he will have a great deal of difficulty in surrendering his will to my will. Otherwise, as you know, the training causes an unwanted burden on someone who is not ready to be trained, or still wishes to follow the enticements of human will."

"I know this Master Ether," the Ambassador replied. Your role is not an easy one, particularly when you must train some special soul. Yet, you are the best. Certainly that is why the Lord of the Stars has made you overseer over the other initiators dwelling on the planet of the angels."

Ambassador Marius paused for a moment and then asked, "Would it seem hasty if I asked when you expect to begin?"

"Not at all Ambassador, I expect to start right away. I will descend to Htrae this day and superimpose my consciousness over that of Sebastian. This will expedite his training. I look at it somewhat like a Vulcan mind meld, my mind to your mind."

Master Ether smiled when he thought of the Vulcan mind meld. Vulcan was a very advanced planet and their people had served as mediators on the Grand Council of Galaxies for many eons. He thought that their ears most extraordinary, but their minds were even more remarkable. But for now, however, other matters were more important. Quickly Master brushed all thought of Vulcan aside and turned to the situation at hand, as Ambassador bid him farewell.

"Then, I wish you well old friend. I am sure that our paths will cross several times before this task is finished, but if not, I look forward to standing beside you at graduation."

"Indeed yes," Master Ether replied. "And I too bid you farewell until next we meet."

Following this exchange, the two emissaries of the Lord of Stars went their separate ways; Ambassador Marius departed for a distant galaxy to stop a planetary war and Master Ether descended to Htrae to begin his new assignment.

As Master Ether entered the lower planes, the dense vibrations, people feelings, emotions and thoughts immediately surrounded him. This had once bothered him a great deal and it was still not pleasant. Nonetheless, as head initiator of the Angelic Kingdom he had endured this many times without complaint. Like Ambassador Marius, he was but a servant to the Lord of the Stars and his reward was the beautiful angels he trained. Now he would begin again.

So many billions of years had passed that only the Lord of the Stars and Ambassador Marius remembered how Master Ether had derived his unusual name. Master Ether, however, was considered one of the greatest beings to ever traverse the ethers where all souls live when they are not in people bodies. In time he had been dubbed *Master Ether,* or one who had conquered the inner worlds. His task not only included the supervision of the unseen universe, but it was also customary for him to descend to any world when he saw some special person struggling to find Lord of the Stars. It was his prerogative to appear to that particular individual on the movie screen of their mind.

After introducing himself, Master Ether then spent months

or even years preparing that particular individual for his or her entry into the angelic kingdom. Thus, as time passed, the Lord of the Stars gave Master Ether the honor and responsibility of assisting in the divine graduation of all planets. Eventually, the Master was promoted from angel to archangel.

Master Ether wasted no time in his search to find Sebastian. Each day the Starians' planet was getting closer to Earth, and Htrae had to reach its full divinity before reaching the closest point of contact with the Emerald Planet's consciousness. There was now an underlying sense of urgency.

Within a very short time the Master landed silently in Sebastian's living room. He saw the future Leader of Htrae sitting in a chair near the window half asleep. In a twinkling of an eye, Master Ether reviewed the memory patterns of Sebastian's soul containing the story of His evolution. When the soul-book had been fully revealed, Master Ether thought, "As usual Ambassador Marius has made a most wise selection."

Suddenly, Sebastian, who was sitting in quiet contemplation with his eyes closed, became aware of a bright light coming toward him and opened his eyes. However, he saw nothing. When he closed them again, the white light seemed to be coming closer and closer. Suddenly, there was a blinding flash and in the center stood the familiar figure of Master Ether. "Good morning Sebastian. This time I have come into your world from the Planet of the Angels in order to teach you the mysteries of divine birth."

Quickly the light and Master Ether disappeared, and Sebastian opened his eyes. Just as before he saw nothing, yet he felt Master Ether's presence.

"I feel your presence Master Ether," said Sebastian, "but I cannot see you. Yet, I want you to know how pleased I am to greet you in my world. I greatly fear that you will have to explain what is happening."

As soon as Sebastian asked the question, he saw himself standing with Franklin in the Elsewhere Land, saying something about his next birth being divine. When that scene disappeared, he was given a glimpse of his future, and he saw himself teaching and preparing the Starians for Htrae's divine mission. Lastly, he saw Earth people hovering in awe and wonder as Htrae drew and closer for its final rendezvous with the graduating planet.

Although Sebastian's nature was generally calm, the beauty of this vision was almost more than he could withstand. He realized that Lord of the Stars had now revealed his final purpose, and that Master Ether had come to prepare him.

The next days were exhausting for Sebastian. By day Master Ether carefully taught the inner mysteries of the world beyond. By night Lord of the Stars revealed the ancient secrets of life and death. Sebastian reviewed his past soul evolution and watched his own birth into human form. This helped him to more fully understand life's strange metamorphosis. "Alas," he thought, "Although the Starians have never forgotten the ways of Lord of the Stars, I can see where the knowledge of our origin did become more obscure. We have been human a very long time."

For a moment Sebastian felt sad about this, but he soon remembered that the entire process was all part of the soul's natural progression. Although he had always understood that human life was not separated from the Lord of the Stars, he now realized more fully that this perfect state of consciousness was not completely manifest in people bodies. It took a divine birth to make it possible for the two natures to become one. Even as the Starian philosopher felt the mighty consciousness of Lord of the Stars rise within him, it became evident that divine birth did not free one from the pains of labor.

As the weeks passed, other Starians were able to sense a change-taking place within Sebastian, and sometimes they would gather around him in the evenings to hear him teach. Other times sadness would fill their hearts, for they knew it would not be long before he would leave them. Sebastian belonged to the whole planet now and the whole needed him much more.

On their last night together, Sebastian looked fondly at Franklin, Sally, Joan, Cedric and all the rest, and said, "As you know, we have spent many epochs together and now I must depart from you for a brief period. As I bid you farewell, I want you to know that it will not be long before we will all be together forever. To be born is to feel separated, but divine birth never again knows a human death and the soul can then continue throughout eternity without interruption."

"Master, we know you are soon to go, but please reveal the mystery of heaven to us." Sally asked quietly.

"Ah, little Sally, we have shared many eons. So, too, we shall one-day share heaven. It is a state of not being, but of becoming all. Though you are, you are not, for the personality of Sally and Sebastian will no longer exist. Each will become united with their counterpart on earth, and then we shall live in divine oneness within Lord of the Stars, enabling all life to live within us. Such is the real heaven."

When Sebastian described the glory of heaven, the Starians saw the radiance on his face and became hushed with awe.

Then, Cedric, the great painter asked, "Are you saying that all states of existence between the people body and pure at-one-ness are but other worlds, seen and unseen, and that none of these are really heaven, although they may appear to be so?"

"Yes, Cedric, but remember, love for the Lord of the Stars is the golden key which opens the door to all mysteries.

"I am sorry my friends," Sebastian said as he stood up, "but I must leave you. Please know that I shall miss you, although I shall always carry you in my heart. And know also, that I shall eagerly wait that time when we shall be together forever. Now, however, because I have been given the secrets of divine transformation, I must give it to others in order for *Operation Earth Angel* to succeed. Each person must fulfill his or her purpose, or the planet's mission cannot be completed. As you know, Htrae draws nearer to Earth every day and we must be ready."

Sebastian looked around the room at his long-time associates with great tenderness and bid them farewell, saying, "Until we meet again."

The Starians watched Sebastian walk through the garden, close the gate, and disappear into the moonlight. During the moment of his departure, a memory returned to each of them of another time, when together they had touched some mysterious moon magic.

Walking along the road, Sebastian also remembered, and turning his gaze up toward the moon, he said, "Well, old friend, it seems that you have not forgotten how to produce your magic through the years. Now I will wander the land as you wander the sky. Come and guide my way, for I will travel with you by night and with the sun by day."

When the Starians could no longer see Sebastian, they returned to the meeting room. Webster was the first one to speak, "Instead of feeling bad, let us ask Lord of the Stars what we can do to hasten the divine birth of Earth. In this way we shall never be separated from our friend, but will share in his work."

Nodding in agreement, everyone pushed a chair into the old familiar Circle of Wisdom. Sitting down, they closed their eyes to begin meditation. After all had become silent, each was surprised to see a white light, and inside the light appeared the old familiar figure of Master Ether.

"Good evening to all of you," the Master said with great kindness, "You must not sorrow for your friend, as you will join him one day on the Planet of the Angels. That time shall come sooner than you think."

With that announcement the Angelic Master disappeared as

suddenly as he had appeared. When the Starians opened their eyes, they felt a great sense of urgency within their soul; as though there was something special each of them had to do.

Even as the Htrae family gathering was going on, some distance away in the forest, Brother Arbo, who had once again retired to the world of contemplation, was rudely awakened. Old Gusty was shaking Brother Arbo's branches wildly.

"Harrumph, Harrumph," Brother Arbo muttered gruffly. "What is it now? You never let me rest in peace."

"I am here to say good-bye," explained Gusty. Then he whispered a strange story into Brother Arbo's branches.

For the first time, the aged tree forgot to act sedately and began waving his branches excitedly. "You mean to tell me that one of my old students has become a Leader!" He shook his branches again. "I always knew there was something special about those Starians, especially Sebastian."

Immediately Brother Arbo regained his normal composure and became his usual gruff self. "Harrumph, Harrumph," he grawked. "That young Sebastian would never have made it without my help."

For a moment Hermano Arbo became silent, and then he said "I never thought I would say this to such a nuisance, but I wish I could go with you. I would like to help Sebastian with his mission."

Old Gusty danced around the tree. "Well, old friend, then you will understand why I have come to say good-bye. I must travel with the young master to keep him company. Don't worry though," he gently added. "I'll keep you posted."

"You old windbag, you are always getting your stories mixed up. Unfortunately, I am a tree, so there is little I can do about the situation. However, you might at least try to keep the details straight just once."

"I will, I will," said Gusty. Then, away he blew toward the golden moon now guiding Sebastian on his journey.

Brother Arbo gazed longingly after him. He wasn't harrumphing or growling any more, but wishing very much that he could follow the wind.

From high above, the Lord of the Stars, as well as Ambassador Marius looked down on Hermano Arbo with deep compassion. Through the silent ether world the consciousness of the Lord of the Stars reached out to the Ambassador. "Do you wish to tell him or should I, Ambassador?"

"It is your surprise, my Lord. You tell him," Ambassador Marius urged.

"Then I shall," and the Lord of the Stars began to speak within the knothole heart of the ancient tree. "You have served me well, Hermano Arbo. And you gave up your freedom more than once to teach people about my ways, although I fear you grumbled a bit. Nonetheless, you heart is good and because of this I am releasing you from your wooden form. This will leave you free to go where you wish. Go, but understand, you must take another form someday, for your work has barely begun."

Hermano Arbo could hardly believe what the Lord of the Stars was saying. At the same time he was feeling something strange and mysterious. He was beginning to feel as light as the wind. Nonetheless, he tried not to get excited and lose his dignity. As he felt himself drift away from his wooden body, the old tree said, "Oh thank you, Lord! Does this mean I can go with Sebastian after all?"

"Why don't you try it and see, Hermano Arbo?" whispered the Lord of the Stars.

At these words, the spirit of the tree moved further away from its wooden shell. Already the leaves had started to wither, but Brother Arbo didn't mind. He was free. Suddenly he remembered Sebastian. "I must hurry," he thought, "or I will get too far behind."

"Gusty," Hermano Arbo called out, "wait for me."

"Highways become the pathways of light," Sebastian sang as he sauntered down the road. For a moment he stopped as he thought about his new freedom and remembered those bound by people bodies, "Ah, soon," he thought, "All of the souls in people bodies will realize that their prisons are made by themselves,"

Without warning, he felt the wind blowing through his hair and the voice of Gusty joining him in song. As he glanced around, he was surprised to notice that every tree along his path reminded him of his old teacher, Hermano Arbo. "Of course," he thought, "one who walks with Lord of the Stars never walks alone. Welcome my friends," he called. "How happy I am that you have come! Let us travel together!"

Sebastian's voice rose in unison with those of Gusty and Brother Arbo as they sang:

This is the story of the rover.
This is our song as we roll along.
We walk the pathway to the stars

In the setting sun of the first day of Great Ones on Htrae, Sebastian rested in the soft grass provided by Mother Htrae and observed the Lord of the Stars playing his endless symphony of creation. Later, as he traveled, Hermano Arbo trained the trees to give shelter to the young leader, while Gusty cooled his brow during the hot summers. Before long, the divine nature of Htrae was felt within all life, and the seventh and final epoch of material manifestation embraced the land.

CHAPTER XIII

Operation Earth Angel

Twenty and seven years passed while Sebastian served as the official Leader of Htrae. His journeys took him over land and sea, and mountains and valleys, always teaching the mysterious ways of Lord of the Stars in order to prepare the Starians for *Operation Earth Angel*. Sebastian taught everyone about the sun nebulas where the worlds of matter are born, and he spoke of the planets in the universe as heavenly bodies. He explained to his students how each of these planetary families served a special role in their own particular solar system.

The teacher also taught the Starians that Earth and Htrae were examples of these heavenly bodies and the purpose of each could not be fulfilled without the other. Those who heard him began to better understand the mission of Htrae, and it was well that they did so. The two planets were scheduled to rendezvous sometime during the following June according to the Starian calendar, just as spring and summer met in their seasonal union.

Although each of the Starians now understood that they must surrender their individual existence to enable people of Earth to become divine they prepared for the end of Htrae happily. As they did so they realized that to fulfill their divine purpose would not diminish either Earth or Htrae, but that both would become more.

The Htraeons would begin to superimpose their consciousness over Earth when the two planets approached their closest point of contact. The Lord of the Stars planned to have Htrae enter Earth's orbital pattern on the sixth day of the sixth month of Earth's solar year. Then, Htrae would continue its descent through the atmosphere above Earth's surface for a period of three days, and complete its rendezvous on the ninth day of June.

As the Starians prepared for the completion of their mission, there was a great deal of speculation taking place on Earth concerning Htrae's nearness. Some of the astronomers felt that the two heavenly bodies were on a collision course, and others felt that Htrae was possibly some comet that would swerve when it hit Earth's gravity field. Although a few scientists were trying to predict the outcome of the great light in the sky, most of those in people bodies on the Emerald Planet continued their day-to-day activities with little concern.

Above earth, beneath a blanket of snow in the early spring of Htrae's last year of existence, final preparations for *Operation Earth Angel* were taking place. The flowers and grasses had just begun to show through the planet's surface in bright green shoots as Sebastian walked along, admiring of the splendor of the coming spring. He stopped for a moment to uncover a little jonquil. He not only felt the nearness of Htrae's end, but he also knew that the time for him to leave the planet was not far away either.

"Ah, little flowers! Like all things, your beauty remains hidden until you give forth the bloom of your final self." he said tenderly. "Even as you strive to come forth, Htrae works diligently to do the same."

Turning, Sebastian called to Gusty. "Come, old friend, and give the jonquil a touch of the warm spring winds! As you know, my work is almost finished. In these last few hours together, let us share the beauty of a new beginning with all we survey."

Gusty did as the master requested, but there was sorrow as he touched the tiny plant. "You do not fully understand what it is like to walk with a master," he sighed. "Yet, I promise that you and I shall always be, for we must help life begin everywhere every spring."

Hermano Arbo nodded in agreement. He knew also that when the master's work was finished that it would also be time for him to continue his own soul progression. Although the soul of the Great Tree had grown in gentleness as he walked with the master, he would still "harrumph!" occasionally when he did not wish anyone to know how he felt. This did not fool Sebastian, who gleefully reminded him of the novelty store in the Redwoods.

While Sebastian walked along enjoying the birth of new spring, Master Ether appeared before him and informed the Starian teacher that the time had come for him to leave. "Sebastian," he said kindly, "Htrae is now prepared for its mission and there is other important work for you to do. You must oversee the final phase of *Operation Earth Angel* and this cannot be accomplished in a people body because it possesses too many limitations."

For a moment, the director of the Angelic Kingdom smiled fondly at Sebastian before continuing to speak. "Come with me and help me carry on the work of the spiritual hierarchy. You can guide the completion of Htrae's mission, as well as Earth's divine birth, from the Planet of the Angels."

"Why thank you, Master Ether. I have felt the time drawing near. As you know, I love Mother Htrae and the Starians very much and I shall miss them greatly. However, I understand that time belongs only to matter and that we shall all be together in the Angelic Kingdom one day."

Sebastian stopped walking, and paused again to observe the miracle of spring. Then he asked, "How much longer do I have?"

The Head of the Angelic Kingdom spoke to Sebastian with measure tenderness and pride, "A few days at the most. Much depends on whether you wish to visit with your old friends before you leave. As you know, Webster, Cedric, Franklin, and the others have also prepared for the end, and each is performing a great work on Htrae. Think about it and then let me know. As always, I am merely a thought away."

"All right, Master Ether, but before you leave, I want to express my gratitude for your help through the years. I know that many of the miracles attributed to me have been brought about by your unseen world. Unfortunately, it is often hard for others to comprehend this. Most of the souls bound to people bodies do not realize how much of their good comes because of Angelic assistance.

"You know," continued Sebastian, as he looked at his long time teacher, "it is difficult to realize that you were once human."

"Sebastian, we were all human at some time or other, though not on your planet. All planets eventually graduate into higher orders if they don't destroy themselves. Even so, death or destruction of a planet can never affect the divine plan existing throughout all creation. The Lord of the Stars is eternal and constant; all other life is subject to change. Now, I fear that I must hasten on my way."

After Master Ether had disappeared in his usual "poof," Sebastian summoned Brother Arbo and Gusty. "My friends, I sense your sadness over my leaving, but you must not feel this way, for we are never truly separated. It is lovely weather, so let us be happy during these final hours together."

As they walked along together, Sebastian thought about returning to visit Sally, Cedric, and the others, but decided against it. "I will appear to them after I have left the body," he thought. "Travel will be much easier at that time." Then he turned his attention to the Lord of the Stars. "Lord of the Stars, I see that the work here is almost finished and I can leave whenever you wish."

Once again Sebastian felt the ever present consciousness of the Great Spirit of the Lord of the Stars moving through him, and he was guided by vision to a distant snow peaked mountain. As he turned in the direction of the mountain, the Lord of the Stars began speaking to him in the voice of a thousand galaxies, although he made no actual physical sound. "Sebastian, you will find a cave at the foot of the great mountain. Go in and lie down on the cool dark floor and rest, while I help Master Ether prepare for your arrival in the Angelic Kingdom. We have a bit of a celebration planned for you on this most auspicious occasion."

Soon thereafter, far away in the Angelic Kingdom, Master Ether laid out a long new white robe, two wings, and a golden crown.

Shortly after Sebastian had left Htrae, Old Gusty carried a tale of the great teacher who had become one with Lord of the Stars. People said that the wind, trees, moon, and sun once paid homage to him. Many believed he never died, for his body was never found, and others claimed that even the flowers filled with blood when he ceased to walk the lands. It is true that a field of red poppies grew at the base of the great White Mountain where he was last seen, and there were times when the sun's unusual glow transformed its glowing peak into a golden shrine.

Sebastian, however, appeared before Sally and the others a few days after he had donned his angelic robes. He spoke to them with great love, saying, "I have departed from Htrae, but you will soon join me, for our work here is almost finished. In order for the other Starians to also complete their work, they must be present when Earth becomes divine. Now, my beloved friends, I bid you farewell, but I will see you soon and we will be together forever." Then he disappeared as quickly as he had come.

Shortly after Sebastian's appearance to them, the remaining six senior members of Htrae joined hands just as they had long ago when they were building their planet. It was a beautiful spring day.

From above, the Lord of the Stars and Ambassador Marius watched as Webster, Sally, Franklin and the others entered the forest. The Starians had seldom gone there after Brother Arbo departed, because the forest was never the same. Since this was to be the last walk on their planet, however, by choice they returned to the place where they had experienced so much happiness.

As they neared the old dead tree, which had once housed Brother Arbo's soul, a voice whispered to them. Looking around, they saw all the trees waving gently in the wind, tenderly reminding them of their old friend. Immediately, at the base of the branches there appeared a very beautiful sight. Before them stood a golden angel with gentle countenance and wings outstretched, his arms open to embrace them. Sebastian had returned to guide them home. As they embraced one another, far away in the Angelic Kingdom Master Ether laid out six more white robes, six more pairs of wings, and six more golden crowns.

Watching the senior Starians graduation ceremony from his heavenly vantage point with the Lord of the Stars, Ambassador Marius said, "You know, My Lord, I shall miss seeing Htrae gleaming in the sun. It has been quite an exciting adventure."

"Come now, Ambassador Marius. Think of the excitement when Htrae completes *Operation Earth Angel* and Earth becomes divine. Neither the Starians, nor those who live on Earth, shall ever be far away from us then. They will have become immortal and we shall always be within them."

Ambassador Marius nodded his head, "Ah yes, of course, all the planets are special, and so there will always be plenty of work. Even now Neptune has had to send negotiators to Mark V, because of its unrest. Nonetheless, I am really quite pleased over the divine birth of Earth. My, the humans of earth are surely in for an amazing adventure."

The Lord of the Star was moved with humor, and replied, "Ambassador, you can rest assured that I am preparing a glorious time for Earth, for they have had a most difficult birth. However," shortly after Earth has graduated a new solar system will be born. I am afraid we shall find ourselves going through this all over again."

"My Lord, I am glad to hear that. Perhaps we could even name one of the new constellations after Sebastian. You know, actually, something like the Astian Solar System sounds rather nice," Ambassador said thoughtfully.

As the Lord of the Stars and Ambassador Marius discussed Earth's divine birth, an announcement was being made on Earth that the planet was possibly doomed. Astronomers, who had been following the movement of Htrae for quite some time, reached the conclusion that Htrae and Earth were on a direct collision course. According to their calculations there would be three days of darkness before the collision, as Htrae passed between the sun's rays and the Earth's surface. Although the matter of the collision received top priority, a solution to avert disaster had not yet been found.

The news traveled swiftly from nation to nation, and the arms race halted. All eyes turned toward the heavens where a bright light loomed ominously above the planet Earth. The heads of all nations, now fearing that the human race was doomed, began to meet with their top scientists to see if something could be done to save Earth. For the first time in the history of the world, everyone worked side-by-side for a common cause. The differences between nations seemed to dissolve. While the scientists were trying to come up with a solution, the Heads of State met at the United Nations. Sometimes they glanced at one another somewhat sheepishly, for the problems of the past seemed small when comparing them to the possible annihilation of their world. Other times they felt the peace of being one brotherhood and they knew that it was good.

At first, of course, the scientists thought that it might be possible to combine the nuclear warheads of all nations and destroy the approaching planet. Although this was certainly possible, at the same time the plan produced a deep concern over radiation fall-out. Many felt that the quantity of fallout would also destroy all existing life forms on Earth, and in the end that would be more painful than instant death. Because it was obvious that the life on both planets was doomed anyway, the Heads of States, along with their scientists, finally agreed that the two planets should be allowed to continue their collision course. Perhaps that way, some small spark of life from both worlds would remain to begin again.

Before long all eyes were turned toward the sky, as everyone on earth watched Htrae moved closer and closer. By day it was like a small sun and by night a round, glowing object, larger than the moon. Then it happened! Htrae moved into Earth's gravity field and darkness fell upon the land.

As Earth neared its end, a great change came over the planet. Nations were no longer at war, the Heads of State worked in friendship, and people sought to comfort each other regardless of their differences. As they did so, these differences disappeared. The humans of Earth finally realized that differences were merely opinions, not necessarily a reality, and they saw that the cause of dissension was of their own creation. The rich began giving to the poor to make their last days more enjoyable, for there was little need of wealth in a dying race. Violence also disappeared, for there was no longer a need for robbery and murder. Every one and every thing would soon be gone.

In the midst of this, the people of Earth found that they cared for one another, and they learned that hate could not exist where there was love. At last the world became what people had been praying for; it had become a land of peace. The people still did not fully comprehend, however, that by bringing their planet to peace they had fulfilled their collective destiny. Now they could graduate and become divine.

Life on Htrae had prepared well for the end, and the Starians sent out an essence of their consciousness to enfold each person on Earth. From its inception, Htrae had, after all, always been a higher reflection of what Earth must become. Nevertheless, the Lord of the Stars could not bring forth this potentiality into being until Earth was ready to graduate and become divine. Now the two planets would meet.

As each Starian voice rose in glorious unison, their light began to pierce every crevice of Earth lest some Earthling remain unprotected and afraid. Every sun and planet in the galaxy also prepared to celebrate the great occasion. The older brothers and sisters of Earth's own solar system, including Saturn and Neptune formed into an alignment. Now they appeared in a straight line above the two colliding planets, making it possible for their collective consciousnesses to transmit both strength and advanced development to Earth in order to aid in Earth's divine graduation. It was a most solemn occasion, and Angelic voices filled the galaxy with song.

The Lord of the Stars was particularly busy during this time, for it was he who had to maneuver both planets into a position of perfect merger. Ambassador Marius, Master Ether and Sebastian stood watching from a nearby planet, each penetrating the consciousness of the Starians in order to give them instructions and insure that *Operation Earth Angel* went smoothly.

On the final day of Earth's human life, the people of Earth awoke to see the descending Htrae almost on top of them. They realized that the end was but hours away. Some went to pray in

their churches; others sat quietly with their favorite books or listened to their favorite music. From sea to sea the land was swathed
in harmony, preparing for its inevitable fate.

During the preceding days, as Htrae had drawn closer and
closer to their planet, the people of Earth realized that their wars
had been unnecessary and that they had spent a great deal of time
on unimportant things. They saw that unhappiness, illness, and
death resulted from their inability to live in harmony with all
living things. Although each human was now trying to accept the
end bravely, they wondered what it might be like to never be again.

The sun produced a glorious dawn for Earth's final phase of
human existence, bathing the planet in rich colors of indigo and
magenta. It was a perfect morning, marred only by the massive
hulk drawing ominously closer to the surface of the planet each
passing minute.

Suddenly it occurred; the two planets collided.

With a great blinding flash of light and with one great explosion, the light of Htrae momentarily blanked out all darkness. In
that same instant, as Htrae merged with Earth, every human being understood the secrets of heaven and earth.

When each person opened his or her eyes, all traces of Htrae
had disappeared. Now their bodies possessed a soft white glow,
which had not been there before. Their heads felt strange also,
and when they looked at each other they saw that their hair had
disappeared into halos of brilliant White Light.

While the people of Earth stood in awe over the miracle that
had just occurred, a great and powerful voice spoke from within
them, a voice without sound. "Long you have journeyed through
matter and searched the reason of your existence. Your struggles
are now over, for that which you have sought so long will now live
within you forever. Know always; your greatest desire has been
fulfilled, for you have earned the peace you once prayed for, and
with it — immortality forever."

The Lord of the Stars paused for a few minutes to observe the glowing planet and then he added, "We welcome each of you into the true universe of the stars and the world of the angels."

From a nearby planet, Ambassador Marius, Master Ether and Sebastian looked at one another with great joy. Then each of them turned toward the nearby asteroid belt, knowing that Earth would never become part of it. *Operation Earth Angel* had succeeded

It was finished. The brother and sister planets of the divine Earth began to move out of alignment, continuing in their famil- iar orbital patterns with the work of evolution. The seventh epoch of earth's progression had concluded, and the Emerald Planet glowed in the morning sun like a great crystal.

The End